Seth was silent, his expression haunted

Lexi's laughter reached them then, drew their attention to the action taking place outside the windows. The little girl's smiling face represented all that was good in the world.

Unprofessional tears threatened. Grace blinked them away, blaming them on fatigue and the emotions that came with returning to North Star and seeing Seth so broken and defeated.

"Look at her. So loving and full of life. You are her example, Seth. If nothing else, your pride alone should keep you fighting, just so you can show her how it's done." He wouldn't look at her, but she was glad to note he didn't take his eyes off Lexi.

"Pride doesn't change anything. I could've walked after that horse threw me if pride had anything to do with healing."

"Then what about responsibility? Would you let Lexi give up? Would you let her stop living if she'd been the one thrown off the horse? Or would you love her so much you'd help her cope? You're only a cripple—" how she hated that word! "—as long as you cripple yourself. It's time to stop feeling sorry for yourself and *do* something about it."

Dear Reader,

Characters are funny beings because they come to writers out of nowhere, take hold of our lives and do not let go until their story is told. After a back/shoulder injury I found myself in physical therapy striving to be stronger and watching the ever-present news channels while I struggled through the sessions. My mind was already using the experience as fodder for a story. I had a physical therapist heroine, a name, a mental picture of her. But what about her past? What kind of life had she led? That was something I still had to figure out.

Over the course of the next few sessions, the news headlines were full of seemingly normal men from seemingly normal lives who'd been arrested or convicted for unspeakable things. And as writers are a sensitive lot, I couldn't get those men or their crimes out of my head. What happens later when those young victims grow up? How do they recover? *Do* they recover? My heroine now had a past, and I had a difficult story to write, both emotionally and spiritually.

Montana Secrets is about secrets, but it's also about forgiveness. Forgiving others isn't always easy, and for Grace it's next to impossible until she learns that acceptance is part of forgiveness.

Montana Secrets is my first published novel and I'd love to hear from you. Please visit me at www.kaystockham.com or send me a note at P.O. Box 232, Minford OH 45648.

God bless,

Kay Stockham

MONTANA SECRETS
Kay Stockham

HARLEQUIN®

TORONTO • NEW YORK • LONDON
AMSTERDAM • PARIS • SYDNEY • HAMBURG
STOCKHOLM • ATHENS • TOKYO • MILAN • MADRID
PRAGUE • WARSAW • BUDAPEST • AUCKLAND

ISBN 0-373-71307-X

MONTANA SECRETS

www.eHarlequin.com

Printed in U.S.A.

To my husband, Chad. I will always love you for believing in me, but more importantly—I love you for telling me to write instead of clean house. Thank goodness you realize there is more to life than immaculate floors.

To my children for being a constant reminder of God's grace. I'm not always sure how to answer your questions, but these things I do know—you'll always be my babies, I'll love you forever and only God knows why He got rid of the dinosaurs.

To my wonderful critique partners and friends who've been with me from the infancy of my writing: Jane, Glenna and Serena; to Jody, Julia and BJo for your friendship and support; and to my editor, Johanna Raisanen, for staying inside on pretty spring days to make this story even better. You are all amazing women and role models, and I'm blessed to have you in my life.

And to romance readers everywhere for loving a happy ending as much as I do. Without you, my stories would never have a home.

CHAPTER ONE

GRACE KORBIT FLINCHED when a book slammed against the wall three feet to the right of her head.

"Next time I won't miss. Get out."

Gathering her courage, she peered into Seth Rowland's bedroom, unable to see much because of the dark blinds covering the windows. Too bad they didn't block the smell. Musty air and a decidedly unpleasant aroma assailed her.

"You gotta hearing problem? None of you've managed to fix me yet and I'm sick of waiting for a miracle."

Grace was shocked. This wasn't the Seth she remembered. Taking a deep breath, she ignored his order and went inside, hoping her instincts would protect her from any additional flying objects. Three steps in, her foot landed on something soft and skidded an inch to the left. *Eeeew.*

But the goo sticking to her foot explained the smell. At least part of it. The pungent odor of a too-ripe banana filled her nostrils. She lifted her shoe,

hobbling momentarily and, using the light stream-
ing in from the connecting bedroom, spotted the
outline of an overflowing trash can. She shook her
foot over the container until she heard a dull *thunk*.

"How about I open the blinds and windows?" she
asked, her voice husky as she scraped the sole of her
shoe over the edge. That done, a steadying breath
full of dust and the lingering smell of fruit propelled
her quickly through the mess.

"How about you go—" Seth finished his crude
suggestion. Grace winced, but she'd heard worse.

She trailed her fingers along the wall until they
found the drawstring pull of the blind and yanked
hard, although she regretted it instantly when the
dust flew. She waved one hand in front of her face
while unlocking the sash with the other. Cold, crisp
air flowed in.

Seth's eyes bored a hole into her back as Grace
made her way to the second window, thankful the
sunlight enabled her to maneuver around the messy
room, which looked as though it hadn't been
cleaned in weeks.

Mindful of the dust, she raised this blind slower,
giving the task more attention than it deserved due
to a sudden nervousness. How had she ever convinced herself she could do this? See Seth again?
Talk to him, *touch* him? But in the same vein, how
could she have said no?

She stared outside, at the dirt-and-gravel road leading away from the house, and knew this was one window she'd better keep closed. Otherwise she'd have a hard time fighting the temptation to climb through and make a run for it.

Unable to postpone the inevitable any longer, she turned. "Seth, I—" Grace gasped at the sight of him and hated herself because she wasn't quick enough to squelch the revealing sound. He heard, too, because his gaze narrowed on her and she knew the exact moment he recognized her—and she realized in an instant Jake hadn't told Seth his ex-girl-friend was to be his next physical therapist.

Seth's eyes widened, then he looked away. But in that moment in between she saw it all. Saw the cold, bitter distance she'd created. The anger and upset and breath-stealing pain.

Seth's guarded stare reminded her of an injured, cornered animal, fighting back out of instinct, but unsure of whether or not he really wanted to continue the battle.

Oh, Seth.

Lucky for her he appeared as shocked to see her as she was to see him in such a condition. She fell back on six years of training and experience. Lessons hard learned and refined by taking on some of the most difficult cases others had given up on. Like Seth.

Squaring her shoulders, she swallowed. "It's good to see you, Seth. Do you throw books at everyone who comes through the door or just me?"

Jaw tight, he continued to glare. "I thought you were— Ah, hell *no,*" he growled as understanding replaced his shock.

She forced herself to move closer with a confidence she didn't feel. "That's right. I'm your new therapist."

Grace crossed her arms over her chest, hoping it looked like a gesture of strength, even arrogance, instead of what it really was—an attempt to control her quivering limbs.

He laughed, the sound gruff and low, sending shivers through her.

Seth glowered at the door. "Jake!"

Moving forward another step, she was amazed at the difference in the man she'd known compared to the one before her. Ten years ago Seth had been clean-cut and entirely too handsome, God-gifted with one of those rugged, craggy faces that only got better with age. Tall and lanky, he'd had a natural swagger and smile that stopped what little traffic North Star, Montana, could lay claim to.

Now the handsome cowboy was gone, and in his place was a bitter and broken man with eyes that burned hot with anger, and an appearance that stated quite clearly Seth didn't care what happened to him. Not anymore.

"He isn't—"

"Jake!" When Jake didn't appear, Seth turned to her. "You've had your look at the cripple, now get out."

Her nails dug into the flesh of her arms. The sharp pain stiffened her resolve and reminded her, for the moment at least, she was the one in charge. She just had to prove it to Seth. And to herself.

"I can't leave you like this."

He laughed without humor. "You didn't have a problem leaving me before. Now's no different."

Now *was* different, but her reasoning was the same. And as badly as she wanted to do as he said, to turn tail and run, she was just as determined to stay.

She shook her head. "I'm good at what I do, Seth. What do you say? Will you work with me?"

A vicious curse filled the air, succinct with fury.

"Fine, I'll leave," she said, careful to keep her voice from shaking even as she raised it to be heard over his ongoing litany. Seth stilled, then smirked in triumph, and that's when she decided he needed a firm kick in the rear. "That is, when you're able to get out of that bed and throw me out yourself."

Neither of them moved. They wound up playing a childish game of Stare Down until finally, Seth bit out yet another long string of curses. "Jake had no right!"

"He's desperate to help you."

Help him? Seth scowled at her. There was no helping him. With every day that passed and every therapist that came and went, the angrier he became, because nothing happened. Nothing. The doctors' diagnoses were wrong.

"You can't." He jerked his head toward the door. "Don't let it hit you on the way out. Better yet, do."

Dust mites floated through the air as she stood there wearing an expression so pitying he wanted to hurl something at her again.

Tall and athletic, Grace still had a natural beauty. Her strength showed in the way her shoulders were squared and braced. The way her chin jutted in determination.

He'd kissed that chin. Run his hands over her body and listened as she sighed, loving the sound and loving her despite the way she'd immediately pull away and establish distance between them. He should've realized she didn't feel the same about him, should've known something was wrong before he'd made a fool of himself.

"I understand your anger at being paralyzed, Seth. I'd be angry, too."

He laughed, unable to quell the bitterness. What a line, that. How could she possibly understand?

Had she ever had to ask for help to take a leak? Endured the indignity of having an audience present for the sole purpose of making sure he didn't fall off the pot the first time he was able to actually use a toilet instead of a bedpan? *No one* understood.

"You don't understand so don't pretend you do. You want to move and you move. You want to walk and you walk. I *don't.*"

"I'm here to help you fix that."

He searched for something else to throw. Not at her, just something to take the edge off. "I don't want you here! You couldn't wait to get out of town ten years ago, but at least you did us both a favor and left before I did something stupid like ask to marry you!"

"I'm sorry," she murmured, her eyes avoiding his. "I should've handled things between us better, but I didn't want to hurt you and I—I wanted to go to college."

"I never would've asked you not to go and you know it. You had a choice, Grace. Two scholarships—a school here where we could've seen each other or a school back east. You made your decision. You left in the middle of the night and ran, as fast and as far as you could, dragging Brent behind you."

"You wouldn't listen to me," she argued. "Things were going too fast. I tried to tell you that—"

He ran a hand over his face. "Any slower and molasses would've beaten us in a race. You made your point. You wanted away from me," he said. "Now I want away from you. You're not welcome here, Grace. Get out of my house, off my ranch and don't come back."

Grace flinched at his words but didn't say anything. Instead of leaving, she approached his hospital bed, making her way through the minefield of books, plastic plates and ranching magazines. Now, there was a kicker. He could read about ranching, but he'd never again be able to do the physical labor he loved so much.

"You have to deal with this," she said, nodding to indicate his legs. "Lying here is getting you nowhere, and I can't leave you like this if for no other reason than what we once meant to each other."

"And what was that?" Seth injected a cruelness into his tone that belied all acknowledgment of their past. He slid his gaze over her again, hoping, praying, she'd go scurrying from the room the way his sister-in-law, Maura, always did. Not Grace though. No, she simply lifted her chin another notch, making him grit his teeth so hard pain shot up to his temple.

He couldn't take his eyes off her, though. Mostly because he was beginning to notice new things about her. Like how her chest rose and fell with her breathing, how she was too thin for her height and her clothes were baggy, as though the weight loss was recent. Shadows stained the skin beneath her green eyes and she looked tired and drawn. Even a bit brittle. As if a good strong wind would make those board-straight shoulders of hers snap.

Had she worried about coming to Montana and facing him after what she'd done? Heaven above, he couldn't help but think she'd never have had the courage to return had he been healthy and whole and the man he'd once been.

He stared at her chest and the fullness there, not giving a rat's ass if he offended her or made her uncomfortable, as it always had in the past. Problem was instead of intimidating *her,* the sight nearly undid *him.*

"You're fired."

"You can't fire someone you didn't hire."

Her voice was husky and rich, tart, like warm, mulled cider on a fall night.

"I'm staying, Seth, and you'd better get used to having me around. The sooner the better."

She followed her brassy warning with a shrug, but the movement was stiff, and now that she stood within reaching distance, he saw a slight quiver to her hands. The twitch of a muscle near her too full lips. Maybe she *was* nervous about facing him. He hoped so, anyway. God knew he had little else to hope for anymore.

"I will make you a deal, though…if you're interested." She propped her hands on her hips, widened her stance.

He almost laughed at the sight. Almost. Because like it or not, he was curious as to what she was offering.

"What deal?"

"I'll leave…if you can beat me at arm wrestling."

Then he did laugh. "You can do better than that, Grace," he murmured, relishing the dark flush that stole over her cheeks at his tone.

Her wide, full mouth pursed. "Arm wrestling is a matter of strength. If you can beat me at that, you should be able to handle your wheelchair fairly well. I'll let Jake know, and maybe if you're lucky, he'll back off on wanting you in therapy. Unless you're afraid to lose."

"I wouldn't lose."

"Then what's the problem?"

She meant it. She actually had the nerve to stand there and taunt him. He sucked in a sharp breath as the red-blooded male in him staggered. Grace was strong, no doubt about it, but he was still bigger, broader, with more than thirty years of ranch life under his belt and enough anger to self-combust. "You'll leave?"

"With bells on."

He stared her down, waiting for her to look away,

fidget, something to indicate she wouldn't hold true to her word. "Fine," he growled. "I'm sure there's a cowbell out in the barn somewhere."

She raised a slim brow. "No backing out, Seth. You have to come with me and give Maura and Jake a chance to clean your room." She looked around, her nose wrinkling, and shaming him even though she didn't say more.

"You've got a deal," he snapped. "Get that table over there and quit stalling so you can leave. You're good at that, remember?"

She didn't comment as she walked over to the adjustable tray that went with his hospital bed and pulled it into position. While she did that, Seth pressed the button that raised the head of his bed, then scooted higher, silently cursing his body when the chore was harder than it should've been. He got himself settled and looked up in time to find her eyeing his legs with speculation.

"I'm going to have to move your legs to sit properly."

He offered a grunt she took as consent, and in a no-nonsense move she grasped his ankles through the sheet and shifted his legs, then hopped up on the bed and sat facing him with her elbow braced on the tray.

"Ready?"

He ignored the glint in her eyes and shoved his

pillow down around his waist to allow him to have maximum stability. Placing his hand against hers palm to palm, he fastened his grip, unwillingly registering the feel of her smooth, cool skin.

"On three," she said, her eyes darting away from his.

Now, *that* reminded him of the teenage girl he remembered.

"One…two—"

"Three."

Her gaze flew to his at his sudden attack, but instead of instantly toppling, Grace held her place with barely a wobble, whereas his burst of strength faded much too fast. Sweat beaded his forehead, slipped down his face and itched when it trickled into his beard.

Seconds passed, not more than sixty seconds tops, and he hated himself more and more with every one of them because he could feel himself weakening. Finally her grip tensed against his, as though she'd been pretending to put up a fight all along, and Grace flattened his arm to the tray without so much as a deep breath to fortify her.

Seth stared at her through the hair hanging over his eyes, ashamed. He'd lost. And chauvinistic or not, he couldn't believe he was such a weakling that he'd lost an arm-wrestling match to a woman. Of all the indignities he'd suffered since his accident, this was the icing topping the proverbial cake.

"Let's get started. I'll get your chair."

"No—"

A mask dropped over her features in preparation for battle. "I'm holding you to your word."

He wondered what she'd do if he simply refused. Jerking his hand out of hers, he raked the hair away from his eyes before gesturing at his legs. "You need to get Jake."

"Why?"

Wasn't it obvious? "You can't lift me into my chair."

"I don't need to lift you." Her tone lost some of its edge. "You'll just slide from the bed to the chair. Besides, you'll help me. Right?"

Why should he?

Because his weight could hurt her.

His nod was slow in coming, but he managed to get the motion out without cursing. He hated this. Hated she saw how weak he'd become.

He was a lost cause. All the other therapists thought so, otherwise they'd have found a backbone and stuck around.

Grace moved his wheelchair next to the bed, then inched the chair closer to the mattress before setting the locks. "Ready?"

No.

"I'll get behind you and—"

"I'll fall." Did she have any idea how much that

statement cost him in pride? He was a man. At least
he used to be, and now he was supposed to let her
lift him in and out of bed? She was too small. Too
thin.

She'd drop him.

Then she'd have to call Jake or one of the ranch
hands he still managed to employ to come lift him
back into the bed like a child. A grown man unable
to get himself in and out of bed. God help him, he'd
been humiliated enough.

"Only if you want to," she said. "I'll have you
from behind. One quick move and you'll be in the
chair. You won't fall because I won't let you." She
got into position at his shoulders. "Trust me in this
if nothing else, Seth, okay? Now, on three." She
laughed softly, the sound wry, her breath warm and
moist on his neck. "No surprises this time, either.
Wait until I say."

Grace planted her feet wide, locked her forearms
under his armpits so that her hands were fisted high
at his chest, and helped him over to the edge of the
bed. Her breasts brushed against his back during the
move, burning his skin beneath the T-shirt he wore.
And despite his anger and embarrassment of the
moment, he was aware of her. Much too aware, all
things considered.

"One…two. Three."

She kept balance for them both while he slid off

the bed into the wheelchair in a surprisingly quick move. He landed awkwardly and had to squirm and shift to straighten himself in the seat. While he did that, Grace put his legs and feet on the supports.

"You're out of practice, but that wasn't too bad, was it?" Grace smiled at him.

He glared at her, hating that she talked down to him. He couldn't handle that from Grace. One therapist had actually clapped his hands and giggled every time Seth had lifted the weights as instructed. He'd lasted two days until Seth had managed to convince the man he'd be better off *giggling* somewhere else.

Grace sighed before she stood, moving around him to unlock the wheels of his chair. Without comment she rolled him out his bedroom door into the hall, the house unusually silent.

"If you're wondering where everyone is, your niece took Jake and Maura out to see the kittens in the barn. Apparently there's one that's pure white, and Lexi's the only one who's able to pet it."

Seth grunted. Lexi loved kittens.

"Here we are. You know you're really lucky to have a setup like this at home."

Seth looked up as they entered what had once been his garage, frowning when he heard the bubbling sound of water. Since his last trip to therapy, a whirlpool had been brought in and set up in the corner.

Another expense. The ranch wasn't solvent the way it used to be and he wondered what Jake had sold to pay for the new equipment. When were Jake and Maura going to get it? All of the expense, the wasted time and energy. It wasn't worth it. *He* wasn't worth it.

"Let's get you settled and get to work."

"Don't waste my time and yours—"

"You have something better to do?" she countered, her expression annoyingly cheerful as she stepped to the side of his wheelchair.

He ground his teeth together and shot her a narrow-eyed look that would once have had any one of his ranch hands scrambling out of his way. Grace didn't budge.

"Come on. On three, just like before." She stood in front of him, her legs braced wide for balance as she bent her knees and wrapped her arms around him to lift him from the chair.

Seth froze when he found his nose buried in her neck, in the silky soft hair at her nape that had escaped her ponytail. She smelled fresh and clean and just like he remembered, like wild flowers and sunshine, musky, warm woman and sweetly scented shampoo.

He slowly raised his head. Sometimes being a man of his word sucked.

CHAPTER TWO

GRACE SWUNG SETH AROUND IN the awkward dance that transferred him to the padded table. Once there, she raised his legs to the surface, her cheeks rosy.

"We're, uh, we're going to be here awhile. Better get comfy."

Seth watched as she scampered away, irritated. He stared up at the ceiling, still dazed to find himself there, and attempted to ignore her movements as she prepared for the session.

The air filled with soft guitar music and he recognized the song as one from a CD in his own collection of favorites, making him wonder if she'd asked Jake or Maura which he preferred, or if they still had similar tastes in music.

Grace drew his attention again as she walked back toward him, her hesitant smile off kilter as she placed a towel and a bottle of lotion on the foot of the wide table where he lay.

"The first thing we've got to do is get you limbered up. I don't suppose you've let Jake help you with your exercises since your last therapist left?"

He just looked at her, silent. What had she done in the ten years she'd been gone? Jake would've told him, could've, since he and Grace had kept in touch, but after the first time or two his brother had mentioned Grace's name, Seth had made it clear he didn't want to discuss her so Jake had pretty much kept Grace's activities and interests to himself from then on.

"O-kay, so we'll start there and move on to a massage."

He ignored her censuring expression and tone and went back to examining the ceiling. It needed a coat of paint, but like everything else around the ranch, it was an expense that had been put on hold because of his injury.

Jake shouldn't have bought the whirlpool. Even though it was used, the cost probably would've covered his quarterly taxes and he couldn't afford to get any more behind.

Grace lifted his left leg and bent it at the knee before pushing toward his chest. He didn't feel it. He wouldn't know she was touching him at all if not for the pressure on his ribs as his thigh pressed in. The irony wasn't lost on him, either. How many times had he kissed her, touched her, and wanted more? Wanted her to touch him? Stroke him as he ached to stroke her? Now here she was with her hands all over him and he couldn't *feel* it.

He laughed, drawing Grace's attention, but he ignored her and closed his eyes, throwing an arm over his face. It was either stare at the ceiling or stare at her. Neither were appealing.

How did someone like him—a rancher used to a hard day's work—deal with being a paraplegic? How did anyone?

The worst was knowing Jake and Maura would never move on with their lives now. He was a burden. An obligation they were duty-bound to care for. Even Grace had felt compelled to help despite the fact she'd left ten years ago and never looked back.

Time passed in a blur of painful recriminations as Grace's determined motions moved him from position to position, the last move placing him on his stomach. Unable to take any more, Seth willed his mind blank and drifted with the sound of the music.

"Time for lunch," she said suddenly. "We'll eat and then get back to work."

He shook his head but didn't raise it. "We're fin—"

"Uncle Seff!"

Lexi's squeal of delight yanked his head toward the door, and he bit back a curse as his niece's white-blond head came barreling toward him.

"Lex—get out of here. Go find your mama," he ordered roughly.

"But, Uncle Seff, you're outta your room!"

The table shook as Lexi scrambled up beside him. He turned his head away from her. "Go to Maura."

Little arms hugged his back and he grimaced. *Baby girl.* Since her birth, Lexi had spent as much time with him as she had with Jake, maybe more, and he hated that she saw him like this. Weak and broken, useless. Had he been an animal, he would've been put out of his misery.

"Hello, Lexi, I'm Grace. I talked to you on the phone, remember? It's nice to finally meet you in person."

"What's wrong with Uncle Seff?"

"Well, your uncle's had a hard workout, honey, and he's not feeling well right now. But once he gets some food in his stomach, he won't be such a bear. I'm sure he wouldn't mind a visit before we start our next session."

"No." What was she doing? "Go find Maura, Lex."

"But—"

"Do what you're told!"

Lexi whimpered and began to cry. Seth slammed his fist against the table, the force behind the blow weakened by the padding beneath. He couldn't handle Lexi's little-girl tears. Or being bombarded with all the questions she'd ask, like why couldn't he walk? Why had he fallen off the horse? *Why didn't he love her anymore?*

"Lexi?" Maura called from somewhere in the house.

"Please, Uncle Seff?"

"In here!" Grace answered before murmuring something soothing in response to Lexi's entreaty.

Seth didn't move, completely humiliated by what was taking place around him. A grown man face-down on a table with his butt up in the air. His neck burned with shame.

"I'm sorry, Grace. She got away from me. We didn't mean to bother you. Did we, Lex?"

"No problem," Grace murmured, her tone warm and soft and vastly different from when she'd spoken so determinedly to him.

"I want him to play with me!" Lexi argued stubbornly. "I been good!"

"Alexandra," Maura scolded, "we've talked about this. And besides, that's not how you behave. Now, I need help with the dessert. Will you come stir the berries, please?"

Disobedient silence greeted Maura's firm suggestion and Seth could imagine the mulish set of his niece's mouth.

"Uncle Seff, *please?* No, Mommy, no! I wanna stay! No!"

His hands locked in abject rage as his niece's compact little body was plucked from the surface of the table, the heat of her gone from where she'd sat pressed against his side. Footsteps sounded, retreating from the room, but if he'd had any doubt that Maura was escorting Lexi away, his niece's pitiful wails put an end to it.

"She's gone," Grace confirmed, censure in her voice. "Did you like making a little girl cry?"

GRACE WAS FUMING BY the time she locked Seth's wheelchair into place in front of his bedroom window.

While they were in therapy, Maura and Jake had performed wonders in Seth's room. The floor was now clean and freshly swept, his hospital bed neatly made, and the air smelled of cinnamon-scented carpet cleaner.

Without comment, she wheeled the hospital tray into position over his lap, trying to gain a fresh perspective to go with the room.

Seth was a normal patient, angry and sad, disillusioned by life's unexpected turn. Everything about this situation was normal.

Except for the fact she'd been in love with him.

"I eat in my bed."

She raised a brow at his surly tone, so hungry she could match his grumpiness with almost no effort.

"Today you don't," she countered, drawing on a nearly empty stock of patience.

"I don't want or need you to babysit me."

"Good, because I—" She broke off when she realized his scowling attention was focused on something happening outside the window.

She followed his gaze and found Jake standing beside the older ranch hand, Hank, who'd driven her from the airport. Both men leaned against the paddock rails and watched as another man worked with a horse.

She glanced back at Seth and found his hands white with strain, gripping the curved arms of his wheelchair. Eyes dark with pain and fury. Envy.

Despite her anger over his behavior with Lexi, her heart softened even though she told herself to stand firm. But to *see* how dearly Seth wanted to be out there—

"Leave me alone."

She closed her eyes briefly and inhaled. "Sorry. There are some medical forms and evaluation sheets I need to fill out with your input. We can share lunch while we get the technical stuff out of the way."

She grabbed a straight-backed chair from beside his bed and carried it to a spot opposite his wheelchair. She lowered it smack dab in front of him so he'd have a hard time ignoring her.

"I'm not hungry."

Seth's stomach chose that moment to growl loudly, and Grace hid her smile when he actually glanced down and frowned, acting genuinely surprised by the noise.

"Maura told me she was going to fix your favorites for lunch. Fried chicken, mashed potatoes, green beans—"

He stared out the window again. "I don't want to eat with you. You got me to therapy this morning. Be happy with that."

"Look, Seth—"

His black eyes fixated on her and it was everything she could do not to flinch. Seth was dynamite ready to explode and she was the match lit to fire.

"No, *you* look—I don't want to eat with you, I don't want to sit with you, I don't want to look at you. *I-don't-want-you-here!*"

Someone coughed quietly, and Grace turned to find Maura hovering in the doorway with a loaded tray in her hands.

Hurt when she knew she had no right to be, Grace waved Jake's pregnant wife inside the now-spotless room and met her halfway, grateful for the distraction and the chance to curb her doubts and memories before they got out of hand.

"Please, don't let him throw it," Maura begged in a hushed voice. "We're out of carpet cleaner."

"Don't talk over me," Seth barked. "I'm right

here, Maura. If you don't want me to throw the damn tray then tell me, not her!"

"S-sorry, Seth. I just—"

"Get out! Both of you, just get the hell *out!*"

Grace forced a smile at the now teary-eyed Maura and took the tray from her trembling hands. "Thank you for all your hard work, Maura. I'm sure Seth will enjoy his favorite foods so much, he won't consider doing anything as childish as wasting it," she said before turning her attention back to Seth. "After all, it would be pretty embarrassing for a grown man to make his pregnant sister-in-law come in and clean his room because of a tantrum, now wouldn't it?"

Seth didn't respond to her scolding and Maura used the break in conversation to duck out the door, wiping her cheeks as she went.

"And I *know* you're not keen on my being here," she continued. "You've made your feelings perfectly clear, but I'm staying…if not for what we used to— to mean to each other, then for Jake and Maura and Lexi."

A gruff laugh escaped him, lacking all traces of humor. "Don't pretend feelings you never had, Grace. And leave my niece out of this."

Feelings she didn't have? Seth had meant everything to her, that's why she hadn't wanted to hurt him. Couldn't bear the thought of him turning away in disgust.

"I won't leave Lexi out of our conversation. I can't because *you* obviously don't know what you're doing to her. Do you *know* how smart she is? A lot smarter than I was at five. Your niece called me in North Carolina to ask me to help you. In fact, she's the one who convinced me to take your case."

"Lucky me."

Grace dropped the tray on top of the hospital table. Maura had placed Seth's meal on hard plastic plates so the action created more noise than anything. The ruckus was worth it when he glanced up at her in surprise.

"Lexi heard Jake on the phone asking me to take your case, and after he hung up, she snuck in and hit the redial to talk to me herself. Just so she could persuade me to come because she wants her favorite uncle to get well."

"You mean she heard you turn Jake down. You told him no."

Unable to deny the truth, she shrugged. "I told Jake I needed time to think about it."

"Afraid to see me again?"

She wanted to look away but couldn't. "Seth, stop feeling sorry for yourself and fight this. I'll help you. And before you say it, I'm *not* leaving. I'm not intimidated by a grown man's temper tantrums."

"My family doesn't need me burdening them," he grated out, his face a dull maroon. "The sooner you and everyone else realize that and move on, the sooner I can have some peace in my own house!"

"Peace?" she asked, incredulous. "Hiding in this room isn't peace, it's giving up! Your family needs you. *Lexi* needs you."

Seth's near-black eyes bared more of his soul than she knew he wanted her to see. "What does she need me for? Wake up, Grace, I'm a *cripple*."

Pain washed over her. Not only Seth's pain, but the pain of every patient she'd come into contact with since beginning her career. "You're her uncle. The *only* uncle she has, and she loves you."

His despair made her want to cry, it touched her heart, breaking through all her training, and through all the barriers she'd erected over the past ten years in an attempt to keep herself from falling for someone as hard as she'd fallen for Seth.

"Don't stand there and preach to me about Lexi."

"Or what?" Seth had so much going for him, and here he was shoving everyone and everything away as hard and as fast as he could. Self-destructing right before her eyes. "Even if you never take another step in your life, you'll always be Lexi's uncle. Nothing will ever change that. Quit feeling sorry for yourself and fight this! Fight back!"

Seth was silent, his expression haunted and brooding. Lexi's laughter reached them then, drew their attention to the action taking place outside the windows. The little girl was with Jake and Hank, her smiling face representative of all that was good in the world.

Unprofessional tears threatened and Grace blinked rapidly to ease the strain, blaming her response on fatigue and frustration and all the emotions that came with returning to North Star and seeing Seth so broken and defeated. She hadn't been eating, hadn't been sleeping. And now when she did close her eyes and sleep, her nightmares were vicious.

"Look at her. So loving and full of life. You are her example, Seth. If nothing else, your pride alone should keep you fighting, just so you can show her how it's done." He wouldn't look at her, but she was glad to note he didn't take his eyes off Lexi.

"Pride doesn't change anything. I could've walked after that horse threw me if pride had anything to do with healing."

She nodded, understanding. Pride certainly didn't even the odds, she'd learned that as well. "Then what about responsibility? Would you let Lexi give up? *Look at her!*" she ordered when his glance left the window. "Look at her and tell me what you'd do if she'd been the one thrown off the horse. Would you let her stop living? Stop playing? Would you let her shove everyone away and hide in her room? Or would you love her so much you'd help her cope? Let her lean on you for strength when she was tired and sad? You're only a cripple—" Lord, how she hated that word! "—as long as you cripple yourself. It's time to stop feeling sorry for yourself and *do* something about it."

"Go to hell."

"I've already been there," she countered with a laugh, the sound emerging from her so bitter and flagrantly pained, she drew Seth's narrowed gaze. Inhaling deeply, she wished she could have taken the words back. Seth didn't know why she'd left him, why she'd run, and he never would.

"All I'm saying is, give that little girl out there some credit. She wants you any way she can get you, and she doesn't care if you walk or crawl or *roll.*"

"Here's the other tray."

Grace turned to find Maura standing just outside the doorway. Reining in her scattered emotions, she crossed the room to retrieve her lunch, but Seth's sister-in-law wouldn't let go of the dishes.

"Don't give up. He'll fight for Lexi if he'll fight for anyone. Jake's always said Seth is as much her father as he is." Maura gave her a hesitant smile of encouragement and released her grip on the food-laden tray.

Grace watched Maura leave the room before she retraced her steps to the chair and sat down. Seth's

stomach growled once again, and he spared her a
glare before his hand shot out and picked up a
chicken leg. He took a bite, another and another, as
if he hadn't eaten in years. At least she'd made him
hungry. Seth's body had recognized the exercise
and extra expenditure of energy even if Seth's
nerves hadn't. But eating once wasn't going to replace the weight or muscle tone he'd lost. Nor give
him the nutrients he needed to fight off winter colds
and flu.

"What about dessert?" he demanded suddenly,
not looking at her. "If Maura made my favorites,
there should be a raspberry cobbler in the kitchen."

She hesitated, noting with no small amount of
surprise that his plate was nearly empty while hers
remained virtually untouched.

"I think she mentioned a cobbler earlier when I
arrived. Want me to go see?" she asked, balancing
her tray on the table by his as she stood. She could
use the time to regain her composure.

Seth shrugged, not looking at her.

"Fine," she said. "Sit tight and I'll be right back."

Seth waited until Grace left his bedroom before
he wheeled himself to the door and shut it as quietly as possible, his fingers hesitating momentarily
before he twisted the lock into place.

Mind made up, he wheeled himself to the door
connecting the spare bedroom to his and locked it

as well before rolling himself back across the room and repositioning himself in front of the hospital tray. His progress was certainly a lot easier thanks to Maura and Jake's cleaning, and like it or not, he was going to have to let them come in every once in a while just so he could get across the floor.

And once he succeeded in getting them to leave?

Not having any answers, he glared down at his plate. His stomach still had a curl of hunger, and he glanced at the door and frowned, wishing he could've gotten his piece of cobbler before locking Grace out.

"Seth?"

The knob twisted until it encountered the lock, and he heard Grace's gusty sigh through the door and all the way across the room where he sat.

"Okay, I get it. We're done for the day," she called, her voice muffled by layers of wood. "I have your cobbler, though," she said in a singsong tone, the one she'd used to tease him way back when.

Despite his anger, he smiled grimly at her obvious delight in withholding his treat. The woman had a mean streak.

"I could leave it out here if you're interested, but then, you'd have to open the door to get it and you never know—I just might kidnap you to finish out your exercises today." She followed the warning with a laugh and then thick silence filled the air, full of expectation.

Seth knew she still stood on the other side of the paneled door. He could feel her. Was aware of her in a way he should have been aware of his lower extremities.

"Seth?"

She said it as if she thought he'd gone somewhere.

"I still need to fill out those papers. Red tape, you know? I'll come by this evening after dinner and we can go through them then. Oh, I almost forgot. You get a rematch tomorrow, bright and early. Better plan your strategy if you plan on winning."

A purely feminine chuckle sounded, capturing his attention and his interest whether he liked it or not. It also grated on his nerves like nobody's business, and he reminded himself she was trying hard to get a rise out of him. The trick was not to play along.

"Can't you just see it? Beating me at arm wrestling and getting me out of your hair?"

He sure could. Which said a lot, considering how long it had been since he'd found himself intrigued by anything. The fantasy of throwing her out of his house held an infinite appeal.

"You know, if you don't say something I just might assume the worst and be forced to come in after you."

He leaned an elbow on the arm of his chair and groaned. After this morning he had no doubt she would do exactly what she said, Jake hot on her heels followed by the rest of the blasted household. A man should have peace in his house.

Contrary to what they believed, he wasn't giving up, he just wanted...to be left alone. To not be a burden. For Jake and Maura to go on with the plans they'd made before his accident and he'd ruined all their lives.

"I'll find a way in."

"Go. Away!"

He heard her laughing at him on the other side of the door. A belly laugh. It reminded him of so many things. So many smiles. He hadn't seen Grace smile much until after they'd begun dating. Then it had become a challenge, discovering what it would take for him to get one of those blindingly beautiful grins of hers.

"All right, then, fine. Have it your way for now. But I'll see you later, Seth. Oh, and go ahead and enjoy my lunch. I'd hate for it to go to waste."

For the first time, he noticed her food and leaned across the table, snatching a chicken wing from her plate. Her loss was his gain.

"While I enjoy *your* piece of hot, gooey, raspberry cobbler...with vanilla ice cream. Oh, *yum.* Seth, this is *sooo* good! Sure you don't want to open the door for some?"

Seth tossed the chicken wing onto the plate with a curse.

CHAPTER THREE

GRACE DIDN'T HAVE THE courage to face Jake and Maura after being so easily outwitted by Seth, so she dug into Seth's slice of cobbler to ease the emptiness of her stomach, and then left the house for a walk.

The barnyard was empty of humans so she ambled in that direction, taking in the landscape she'd missed more than she realized. White-capped mountains towered in the distance, and overhead, blue, cloud-spotted Montana sky stretched on forever. Big-sky country was a sight to behold. Beautiful and humbling due to its sheer size alone.

Brent missed Montana so much. When she'd taken her younger brother with her to college on the east coast, he'd been sullen and angry, upset that she'd disrupted his life so drastically. At the time she'd been desperate to get away, to discover who she was out of North Star. But now as she looked out at the landscape she better understood Brent's behavior and what she'd dismissed as teenaged angst.

Grace breathed deep and let the crisp, fresh air ease the tension lining her shoulders. Maybe returning to North Star wouldn't be so bad after all. Maybe her shrink was right and the nightmares she'd been having ever since Jake had called to ask for her help would dissipate once she'd settled in and realized nothing here could hurt her anymore.

Horses roamed in the paddock, and she leaned against the metal bars, glancing around at Seth's large log home and outbuildings as the scent of horses and hay and manure converged in the air. Corn stalks gathered in a mass and tied with twine decorated both sides of the porch steps, the bases layered with pumpkins, mums and gourds. A scarecrow guarded the front door, wearing a red bandanna and cowboy hat, and to the left of the house, a colorful witch had flown into a tree. The poor witch's arms and legs stuck out in front of the tree while her broom and hat jutted out from behind. She smiled at the sight, having a good idea what it felt like.

A distant sound caught her attention, and as she watched, the screen door opened with a squeak and closed with a bang after Seth's niece ran out.

The five-year-old slowed down long enough to maneuver the steps, pausing at the bottom and looking over her shoulder when the screen door opened again. This time Seth's brother, Jake, and his wife,

Maura, exited, and Grace straightened, attempting to prepare herself for the conversation about to take place.

She and Jake had been friends a long time. Ever since Todd Burchett had cornered her against her locker in high school and tried to steal a kiss. Jake had stopped him, and from then on, kept an eye on her like a protective older brother. Through the years their relationship had undergone changes, especially when she and Seth broke up, and again when Jake had married Maura. Their e-mails had become fewer and farther between, down to an e-card at Christmas and every now and again a birthday when they weren't too busy to remember.

Lexi took off ahead of her parents, running toward her as freely as only a child could run. The horses drew her interest and the little girl climbed onto the paddock rails beside Grace.

"Hi."

"Hi, yourself."

"He locked you out, didn't he?" Jake demanded bluntly once he'd come within talking distance.

All she could offer was a tense smile. "How'd you guess?"

Maura shook her head as she smoothed the material of her navy maternity blouse over her rounded stomach and held it in place when it threatened to blow up in the breeze.

A trace of envy stabbed deep, then disappeared. Grace was happy for Jake and Maura. Thrilled Jake had done so well for himself. But sometimes, like now, she wished for more, too. More of a life, a special someone. A child. She could have had it all with Seth.

Except she'd run away instead.

"I'm sorry, Grace. I thought with you he'd do better." Jake glared at the house in obvious frustration. "I'll go talk to him."

Grace shook her head. "No, it's okay. He needs time to get over his surprise at seeing me. I just sort of blew in and bullied him into therapy because I was anxious to get our first confrontation over with. We'll work this out on our own."

"You think you can get him to come around?" Maura asked hesitantly before exchanging an indecipherable look with her husband. "Grace…now that you're here…you should probably know you're Seth's sixth therapist."

"Sixth?" Nerves rapidly returning, she remembered her first glimpse of Seth's room and rounded on Jake. "There were only two therapists listed in his file. You *said* you'd hired them while you waited for me to finish up with my last case."

"I, uh, figured what you didn't know wouldn't hurt you," Jake told her, his expression sheepish. "Besides," he added quickly when she opened her mouth. "I knew you'd get all the information when you got here, so what was the harm of holding just a little back?"

"A little? Five therapists is a little?"

Jake planted his hands on his hips and nodded. "I didn't want to scare you off. Not when I knew how hard it would be to get you back here considering how things ended between you two."

Much as she hated to admit it, Jake was right. Had she known the extent of Seth's difficulties and mood, that she would be *sixth* in a long line of therapists who'd already called it quits, she probably would've used them as an excuse not to take him on. No wonder Seth was so upset. He was probably giving up hope himself. But if five therapists had come and gone, what made Jake think she could do any better?

Maura stepped closer. "You will stay, Grace, won't you?"

Grace stared into the woman's pixie-ish face, her strawberry-blond curls blowing in the breeze as her blue-green gaze pleaded with hers to do something about her present situation. Until this morning she'd never met Maura, never even spoken to her on the phone, and yet in that instant a bond formed.

"I can't work miracles."

"No, I realize that," Maura said quickly, "but you're already here. You've unpacked. Please stay."

Maura's desperation called to her and she let out another gusty sigh. She stared at the house, at Seth's windows. Maybe she'd come full circle. She'd left North Star with little money, a broken heart and more bad memories and baggage than any one person should have to carry—and now she'd returned with basically the same.

"Grace, I should've told you about the others, but—my only excuse is that I was afraid you'd back out, and after seeing Seth today, you can understand why we're so desperate. Maura and I talked about it, and we thought maybe you could help him fight this."

Maybe, maybe not. Seth was on the brink of something, but what? Her professional opinion was that he could go either way. Hit bottom and realize the only way out of his present situation was up, or hit bottom and never return.

"I'll need to review all of the notes from those therapists you didn't tell me about," she murmured without taking her eyes off Seth's window.

"The file's in my office ready for you."

She blinked, looking back at Jake. "And Seth will have to come around or else I *will* move on so you can find someone who can get through to him before—" She broke off, acutely aware of Lexi's presence beside her.

"That's fine." Jake's dark expression mirrored her concern.

"I don't want you to go," Lexi chirped, proving she had indeed been listening to their conversation. The little girl turned sideways on the rails and held on with one arm, wrapping the other around Grace's neck and hugging. "You just got here and I like you better'n all the other therapists."

Grace laughed at Lexi's comment and Jake's co-inciding wince. "Well, considering there were so *many* of them, I'll take that as high praise, Lexi. Thank you."

Obviously relieved, Maura leaned against a sup-porting metal post and sagged, her eyelids droop-ing as she rubbed the small of her back. "Thank goodness," she said with a smile. "It'll be nice to have another woman around. There's entirely too much testosterone on this ranch, and the parade of male therapists going through didn't help."

Jake wrapped an arm around Maura's shoulders and pulled her against his side, and Grace realized exactly how pregnant Maura was. She straightened. "Maura, please don't feel as if you have to entertain me. I'm used to being on my own when I'm not working with a patient. You don't need to keep me company if you don't feel up to it."

Maura's cheeks colored as she yawned again. "Oh! I'm sorry, I don't mean to be rude—"

"You're not rude, you're pregnant," Grace in-sisted. "And pregnant women need lots of rest. Especially after a day like today. You've been on your feet since I got here."

Jake rubbed his wife's shoulders and dropped a kiss on her cheek. "You want to go lie down? I'll keep an eye on Lexi and show Grace around."

Maura's forehead wrinkled with a frown. "You can't. You've got to run over to see Phil Estes, remember?"

He grimaced. "Aah, no, I forgot all about that."

"Phil's an accountant," Maura explained, closing her eyes and sighing as Jake continued to massage. "Jake and Phil are swapping legal advice for accounting advice."

"I'll watch Lexi," Grace offered.

"Really? Thanks, Grace," Jake said.

Maura's eyes popped open and she shook her head at her husband's quick acceptance. "But we couldn't possibly— You just got here and you've got to be as tired as I am after catching such an early flight and then dealing with Seth. Thank you, Grace, but we couldn't impose," she said, sliding Jake a chiding glance. "We didn't ask you to come to babysit."

"I know that," Grace said with a wink at Lexi's hopeful expression. "But this way Lexi can give me the tour of the ranch from her eyes."

"Yeah, yeah! I'm too big for a nap," Lexi said. "And I want to show Grace the kittens 'n' Pebble 'n' Eeyore—"

"Eeyore?" Grace's smile widened as she watched the little girl's excitement grow.

Lexi giggled again, nodding rapidly. "He's a donkey and he's got great big ears! Bigger'n normal. An' Pebble's my pony."

"*Oh,*" Grace said, loving the expression Lexi wore as she described her friends. What was it like to be so innocent and carefree? At Lexi's age she was already more than a little world-wary, having listened to her mother and the man she'd thought was her father fighting for so many years.

"Well, looks like you two will get along great." Jake flashed Grace a thankful smile over Maura's head.

"But— Grace, are you sure?"

"It's no problem, Maura. Really."

"They'll be fine. You go lie down and get off your feet," Jake ordered, squeezing Maura's shoulders one last time. "I'll be back in a couple hours, and if you've managed to sleep that long, I'll free Grace then. How's that?"

Maura nodded hesitantly as Lexi jumped to the ground and hopped up and down. The child grabbed Grace's hand and began tugging. "Let's go see the kittens!"

Grace slowly let Lexi pull her toward the barn. "Maura, go rest. We'll be fine. And stop worrying because I don't mind at all."

Jake shot a stern look at his daughter. "Be good, brat."

"I will," Lexi promised. "Come on, Grace!"

"If you need to get into Seth's room, there's a key hanging inside the kitchen cupboard by the refrigerator," Jake called, his voice echoing against the barn's surface. "Lexi can show you."

"That's where Uncle Seff can't reach it."

Grace paused long enough to glare at Jake, ignoring Lexi's tugging hands. "Locking the door is normal, too?"

Jake shrugged, sheepish once again. "When we've refused to do what he wants, yeah, he locks us out. I'll check on him before I go to Estes's house, but if the doors are still locked when you go in, don't be surprised. Just give him some time. He unlocks them when he gets hungry."

Grace nodded, her thoughts once again focused on the man inside the house. What else hadn't Jake told her?

"Grace, come on!"

She looked down at Lexi and playfully pulled her hand free. "Race you there!"

Lexi squealed with excitement and took off running. Grace slowly sprinted after her.

Maura laughed, her hand still rubbing her lower back. "Oh, you two are making me tired just watching you! Have fun! And Grace? Thank you!"

Grace waved and followed Lexi around the paddock fence to the open barn doors and inside.

"The kittens're in here," Lexi said, leading the way past empty stalls to the tack room in back.

Grace's footsteps halted as she looked around, remembering the high school graduation party Seth had hosted for Jake. She'd hidden away in the shadows of the barn to watch it all, overwhelmed by the freedom of being able to move and eat and talk without fear or repercussions.

That's where Seth had found her. He'd walked in to check on a mare nearing to foal and seen her in the shadows. Before long Grace and Seth were both in the stall with the mare, talking as though they'd always been friends instead of virtual strangers.

"Grace, back here! The mommy is all black wiff white feet. Like socks," Lexi informed her, her expression all-knowing as she waited impatiently. "And all the kittens are black with socks, too. 'Cept for one. It's all white with a black nose. The mommy don't like it."

"She doesn't?" Grace entered the tack room behind the little girl.

"No, she don't like it," Lexi repeated, her face sliding into a deep frown as she looked around the room. "'Cause it don't look like her." She peeked at Grace from beneath her lowered lashes. "Like I don't look like Uncle Seff."

Startled by the comparison, Grace sank to her knees on the planked floor to be at eye level with the little girl, snagging a stray tendril near Lexi's bow mouth and curling it behind her tiny ear. "You don't look like your daddy, either, but he loves you, doesn't he?"

Lexi shrugged. "He has to 'cause he's Daddy."

Grace smiled at the simplicity of the child's words, knowing all too well how untrue that statement could be. Earl Korbit wasn't her father and Grace certainly didn't mourn the loss. But the man whose DNA ran through her veins hadn't hung around, either. Daddies didn't always love.

"Well, honey, sometimes cats do strange things and it can't be helped, but your uncle Seth isn't like that. And he does love you even though—"

"Uh-uh." Lexi's chin came up and a scowl very much resembling her uncle's covered her face. "He don't. He won't play with me now and I think it's 'cause I look like my mommy and Aunt Arie and it makes him sad 'cause she died."

Grace caught her breath at the tears sparkling in Lexi's dark blue eyes. Lexi thought Seth didn't like her because she resembled Maura and her aunt?

Sisters, she remembered abruptly. Seth had married Maura's half sister. Oh, how it had hurt to hear the news. Sad, jealous and miserable, but happy for him. And then aching for the pain he suffered when she'd heard Arie had been killed in an accident three years ago.

"Well, if you want my opinion, I think right now you look very much like your daddy and Uncle Seth."

"Really?"

"Really," Grace reassured her with a smile. "In fact, I'm quite positive I saw that *exact* look on your uncle's face this morning when I went in to take him to therapy."

Lexi's shoulders drooped. "But not my hair and eyes?"

Grace tugged on one of Lexi's white-blond curls, so opposite of Jake and Seth's dark hair and coloring. "No, not those but—"

"Uncle Seff's sad."

A world's worth of hurt and sadness were revealed in the little girl's statement, and Grace sank back onto her heels. Lexi helped herself to her lap, wrapping her arms around her neck and hugging until the child's pointy chin dug into the tender muscles of Grace's shoulder.

"Yes, he is, honey, but I promise it's normal. Wouldn't you be sad if your legs didn't work?

The child nodded. "Grace?"

She rubbed Lexi's back in small circles. "What?"

"Think Aunt Arie's in heaven?"

"Why do you ask?"

Lexi squirmed but kept her face buried in Grace's neck. "I don't know. Just 'cause maybe if she come back then Uncle Seff would be happy again."

Grace squeezed the child in a gentle hug, ignoring the pain stabbing her heart. If Arie were still alive, no way would Grace have accepted the job as Seth's therapist. Knowing he'd loved someone else was one thing, seeing it another. "Honey, when people die they—they go to heaven. They don't come back. And I think you need to be talking to your mom and dad about this instead of me, don't you?"

Lexi shrugged, her shoulder bumping Grace's chin. "They won't talk 'bout her. Uncle Seff used to take me to the cabin and let me play with her things, but that made Mommy 'n' Daddy fight. Now he can't do that, anyway 'cause his legs is broke."

"The cabin?" Grace asked, desperate to change the subject. Why would Jake and Maura be angry over Seth helping Lexi remember her aunt? Because it was too painful?

Lexi nodded. "She liked to paint. Me, too. Mommy lets me fingerpaint."

"That sounds like fun."

Lexi drew back to look into her eyes, her arms still looped around Grace's neck. "It was Aunt Arie's stu—stu—"

"Studio?" she asked, catching on.

Lexi nodded and her ponytail bobbed. "Yeah.

Uncle Seff and Daddy took all her pictures out of
the house. There's one in my room, though, 'cause
she made it just for me after she painted my room."

A flash of white caught Grace's eye just then and
she glanced over Lexi's head to see a white kitten
scampering out of the way of a much larger white-
socked black paw. A large black cat appeared next,
hissing angrily before ducking her head back behind
a box in the corner where Grace could hear varying
tones of young *meows.* The white kitten looked
longingly at the area where the mama cat had disappeared.

Lexi sighed. "See? She don't like it."

No, she didn't, but at least it ended the subject at
hand until Grace had a chance to mention Lexi's
comments to Maura and Jake. On the other hand,
one look at the shaking, pitiful creature proved it
needed to be fed, and she hated to think of something happening to the kitten after all the upset in
Lexi's young life.

"You know, the kitten looks really hungry. Why
don't we take it into the house and get it some milk?
Maybe it'll drink it."

"Okay." Lexi stood and walked over to the ball
of fluff. The kitten crouched down but didn't run,
and Jake's daughter scooped up the animal and cradled it against her chest with a murmur. Obviously,
the kitten knew when it had a good thing, because

it stuck out an impossibly pink tongue and licked Lexi's chin as though in thanks.

"That tickles," the child said with a giggle.

Grace laughed as well, hoping Lexi wouldn't notice how strained the sound appeared. "Come on, let's go see if she'll eat." She got to her feet and brushed the dirt from her knees, straightening to see Lexi's answering smile waver.

Uneasy, Grace turned and found a man leaning against a wall behind them, watching them, and from the looks of it he'd been there for a while. She stiffened, angry with herself because her instincts were usually better. But she'd been so rattled by Lexi's conversation, it was no wonder she hadn't realized they had an audience. An audience that looked vaguely familiar.

"Hello," she said, and waited for the man, one of the ranch hands she'd seen earlier with Jake, to speak.

"Ma'am."

The man was older than her by a good twenty or thirty years, in his late forties, early fifties, with deeply tanned skin and sun-bleached hair. His work clothes were worn and faded from washing. His hat, dusty and stained with sweat, was in his hand. The man pushed himself away from the doorjamb and Grace's heart picked up its pace at the close confines since he blocked the only exit.

"Heard Seth got a new therapist," he murmured, smiling as his eyes trailed over her lazily. "You're Earl Korbit's daughter, aren't you?"

Her skin crawled at the connection, but she nodded, swallowing. People knew her as Earl's daughter, but correcting them would only cause more speculation. She let it be.

"Her name's Grace," Lexi provided.

"Roy Bernard," he said, ignoring Lexi entirely as he looked Grace up and down again. "I think we've met a time or two. Been to your house to pick your dad up for work."

Grace didn't comment, wondering why she was shocked to run into one of Earl's friends. He'd liked to drink, to party, and had had numerous hunting buddies come and go through the years. Bernard must have been one of them.

She'd steered clear of them all anytime Earl and his cronies were at the house. Tried not to draw attention to herself. At least Earl had watched out for her that way and made sure none of his friends bothered her.

"We came to see the kittens."

"Yeah? Well, they've missed you." Absently, the ranch hand reached out and ruffled Lexi's hair.

Grace shifted, uncomfortable with the man's stare. Her instincts might have failed her earlier, but they were going crazy now. And even though the ranch hand hadn't done a single thing wrong, something wasn't right. Her mind raced, and all the emotions behind her tormented thoughts made it nearly impossible to breathe.

Grace lifted a sweat-dampened hand and rubbed her temple as it began to throb. "Lexi, we need to go. Mr. Bernard has things to do and that kitten needs to be fed."

"No, ma'am—that is, I enjoyed watching the two of you play. Pretty scene."

Heat flared in his eyes. Lust.

Her imagination.

Bernard hesitated, then stepped slightly to one side. "You girls go ahead. I've gotta get a new halter." He indicated the corner of the tack room with one hand.

"Come on, Grace."

Grace walked toward the door, trying her best to ignore the ranch hand. Chalking her reaction up to fatigue, she exited the tack room behind Lexi, her shoulder brushing against Bernard's chest as she slipped through the opening. A shiver slithered down her spine, overriding all the excuses in her head.

"Bye, Lexi," Bernard said suddenly. "You come back and see me again, okay? And make sure you bring Grace. I'd like to be her friend, too."

Lexi turned and gave the man an innocent grin. "Okay! Bye, Roy. See ya later!"

Bernard nodded at Grace, an odd smile on his face that made her want to break out into a run.

"Come on, Grace, hurry!"

She picked up her pace and followed Lexi along the stalls. The look in Roy Bernard's eyes stayed with her, though, and she blamed being back in North Star and Bernard's claim to knowing her step-father.

"Think Uncle Seff'll be mad? Daddy says it's his house and we just live there."

Grace latched onto the change in subject, gratefully shifting her thoughts away from the darkness of her mind. "We'll have to see, won't we?"

Given his mood, Seth probably wouldn't even notice the kitten. Unless she told him. Which, she mused with a spark of devilry, might well get him riled up enough to care about the events going on around him if only for an afternoon.

"If he is mad, I'll tell him it was my idea, okay? I'll take full responsibility so you won't get in trouble."

Lexi nodded, but the expression she wore said all too clearly she was worried about the outcome. "He'll pro'bly yell," she offered timidly.

"Yup."

"Maybe throw somethin', too."

"Maybe."

Lexi peeked up at her but kept walking, making

no offer to leave the kitten outside and bring the milk to it. "He don' scare you when he yells?"

"Nope. People yell for a lot of reasons, but the trick to keeping your feelings from getting hurt is to ignore anything bad they say or do."

"Like when Bobby Lawson pokes me in the back at Sunday school?"

"Just like that," she agreed.

"I can't wait to show Uncle Seff!"

Grace smiled weakly. Maybe the cat would eat slowly. She'd need the time to think of the perfect way to inform Seth he now had a house pet.

SETH WAS ASLEEP IN HIS wheelchair when he heard the scrape of a key in the lock. He jerked up as the door swung wide, and blinked as Grace walked in with a file tucked under one arm, a loaded tray skillfully balanced in her other hand.

"Ouch. That can't have been a comfortable nap. Guess I'll have to remember not to leave the room from now on until our sessions are *completely* over."

He grunted in response, watching as she replaced the old tray with the new, then held the manila folder to her chest as if it were a shield. A muscle at the corner of her too-full lips ticked.

"Something wrong?"

"No," she said quickly, licking her lips and waving a slightly trembling hand in the air. "But Lexi's coming in to see you, and…she's bringing a friend."

"I already told you I don't want to—" He cursed. "What'd you say?"

Grace nodded. "She can't wait for you to meet him."

"Him?"

An audacious glint appeared in her eyes as her chin lifted. "Since you were hiding in here, I told Lexi she could bring the kitten in from the barn." She smiled, drawing his interest and irritating him to no end. "Hope you don't mind."

Not mind an indoor pet that would have to be house-trained, fed and cared-for?

"Did you ask Jake and Maura since they'll be the ones looking after it?"

A nonchalant shrug was his answer. "They were both occupied."

She couldn't be that obtuse. A kitten with claws and odor and hair and she didn't ask? "You took everyone being *busy* as a sign to give Lexi permission to upset the household?" He would have said yes—he could never refuse Lexi anything—but the fact Grace had allowed Lexi to do something so drastic without getting permission from him or anyone else—

"It's only a kitten." She tilted her head to the side. "And you were locked in here hiding."

"I was not *hiding!*"

"How could I ask? If you want a say in the matters concerning your household," she taunted, her gaze narrowing on his, "I suggest making yourself available in the future."

"You knew exactly where I was."

"But you didn't want to be bothered."

"That doesn't give you the right—"

"Uncle Seff! Uncle Seff, look!" Lexi ran through his open bedroom door with a white kitten clutched to her chest in a stranglehold the animal surprisingly tolerated. "Uncle Seff, see? This is Blacky."

"Blacky?"

"Don't you see his black nose?" Lexi demanded as she pointed to the area in question.

The tiny black spot on the kitten's face was so minuscule it would likely turn pink within a day.

"He likes milk an' the mama cat won't feed 'im an' he's scared in the barn by hisself an' can I keep 'im? Please? Mommy an' Grace said I had to ask you."

"Lexi, honey, your uncle has decided—"

"You can keep him." Seth shot a quelling look in Grace's direction. He'd been had. She'd deliberately made him think the kitten was a done deal just to rile him, and he didn't like it. He didn't like it at all. Jaw locked, Seth frowned at Grace.

"Yay!" Lexi jumped up and down in excitement. "I can keep 'im, I can keep 'im!"

Seth winced as the kitten's head and body bobbed up and down in Lexi's jiggling arms. He bit back a gruff laugh. "Take it easy or you'll strangle him, Lex."

She stopped jumping. "I've gotta go tell Mommy you said I can keep 'im!"

"Only if you take care of him. He's your responsibility, and your mama has enough to handle right now getting ready to have the baby. She can't be taking care of a cat on top of everything else around here."

"I know! I will! Thank you, Uncle Seff! Thank you, Grace!" As fast as Lexi had run into the room, she was back out again, her ponytail bouncing behind her.

"You just made her day," Grace murmured softly.

He turned his attention away from the empty doorway and focused on the woman in front of him. "You deliberately let me think you'd already given her permission to keep the cat."

She tossed him a satisfied smile, one that lit up her features and softened the angles of her face. "What did it feel like?"

"What did what feel like?"

"Caring about something again? Enough that you actually forgot about your present circumstances long enough to concentrate on something else?"

He rubbed a hand over his thick beard and glared

up at her. "Don't do anything like that again, Grace." He refused to acknowledge her question. "If everyone's busy and Lexi needs anything—consult me. Better yet, leave and it won't be a problem at all."

"Quit locking people out and beat me at arm wrestling and I will."

He snapped his mouth shut, grinding his teeth as he shook his head at her and himself. What was it about her that made him want to regain the strength he'd lost just so he could prove to her he was still a man? Prove to her he could still kiss her senseless and more if she'd just let him.

"Sit down," he ordered abruptly. "I hate looking up all the time."

Without comment Grace snagged the tray from the seat of her chair and made herself comfortable. "I'm going to eat with the family tonight, so while you eat, I thought I'd fill out those papers we talked about earlier."

Knowing she wouldn't fall for his trick twice, he picked up his fork and dug into his food. "Suit yourself."

Silence settled in around them, and after a second's hesitation, Grace began writing. She paused every now and then to ask for specific information. His social security number. What level of pain he felt.

Now, there was a joke. Pain would be preferable

to the big fat nothing his legs represented now. He finished eating before Grace completed her paperwork, so he sat back in his wheelchair and watched her.

With her hair pulled back in a neat ponytail, Grace looked like the teenager he'd known."Remember that night in the barn?"

Her head tilted to the side and the pen in her hand wobbled before she abruptly began gathering up her papers and stood, clutching the folder to her chest once again. "These are nearly finished. I don't need help with the rest, so I think I'll go give Maura a hand in the kitchen—"

So she could push him, but not the other way around? "I'm not going to therapy, Grace."

The starch reappeared in her shoulders as she turned and stalked toward the door. "Life's funny, don't you think?"

"Hilarious."

"I'm serious. I never took you for a coward, but—"

"You little—"

"—you're acting like one."

"Come back here and say that," he ordered.

She paused in the doorway, a thin brow arched high. "I will, but in the morning. I'm up for the challenge. Are you?"

CHAPTER FOUR

"UNCLE SEFF DOESN'T COME out to eat with us," Lexi murmured, a thoughtful frown on her face as she carefully picked a pink crayon from the box in front of her.

Grace sat on a pillow on the floor across from Lexi, absently coloring the picture the little girl had chosen for her. "You miss playing with him, don't you, honey?"

Lexi nodded, not looking up. Maura stood in the kitchen stirring something on the stove, and Grace was surprised to note her expression. Anger, upset. Frustration. Maura's face revealed a range of emotions, none of them particularly pleasant or healthy given her pregnant state.

Grace turned her attention back to the child. "You know, Lexi, sometimes it's hard to accept being hurt. And when everyone else around you behaves as they always did, walking and talking and working, it makes it even harder for your uncle Seth not to be able to do the same."

Lexi stopped coloring, her big blue eyes dark with concern. "Can you make him better?"

Considering she'd already been locked out of his room, given a thorough put-down regarding her boundaries where his niece was concerned, and ordered not to bother him about therapy in the morning, she wasn't so sure. "I'm going to try."

"But what if he don't ever walk?"

She glanced at Maura once again, wishing she were in the kitchen with her instead of being put on the spot. Maura stood within easy hearing distance, and either she wasn't paying attention or she simply chose not to join the discussion due to her feelings regarding Seth—whatever they were.

Grace sighed, set her crayon down and leaned against the couch behind her. "Well, if he doesn't, will you not love him anymore?"

Lexi shook her head, her curls bouncing. "I'll always love Uncle Seff. He tooked care of me when Mommy and Daddy both worked."

Grace smiled at her. "That's all that matters, then, isn't it? I'll do my best to help him walk, but if he can't, you'll love him, anyway. We'll make a good team."

"But I want him to get better now."

"I know you do, honey. We all do, but it takes time." Grace tried to think in terms the child would understand. "Have you ever fallen down really hard and had the breath knocked out of you?"

"Uh-huh. One time when I tried to roller-skate. I fell down and cried 'cause I couldn't breathe."

"So after you stopped crying, did you get back up and skate right away?"

Lexi shook her head firmly. "But I did later," she added.

"Well," Grace said, picking up her crayon to color again, "your uncle's sort of like that. He's had the breath knocked out of him and he's sitting in his room waiting until he's ready to try again. It's just taking him a while longer than it did you."

She didn't know if Lexi understood her explanation or not, but the child went back to coloring her picture without further questions or comments.

The front door opened and shut with a bang. "Anybody home?"

"In the kitchen!" Maura wiped her hands on a towel.

Grace watched as Jake walked directly to his wife and dropped a kiss on Maura's mouth before wrapping an arm around her shoulders and palming her stomach. "How's all my girls?"

Lexi giggled. "Grace's not your girl. Just me'n mommy'n baby."

Jake chuckled and continued to rub Maura's pregnant belly. "Well, I suppose you're right. But Grace and I have been friends for a long time so she'll have to be my girl until she finds somebody to claim her."

Grace raised a brow at Jake's statement. *Claim* her? Not likely.

"She can marry Uncle Seff!" Lexi exclaimed. "You told Mommy they used to like each other. Uncle Seff'll have a wife and a therapist, too!"

Grace glanced from Jake's amused features to Lexi's hopeful expression. "Lexi, honey, therapists don't marry their patients."

"Why not? Don't you like Uncle Seff?"

"Well, Grace?" Jake prodded, his eyes twinkling. "Don't you?"

"Jake, hush," Maura scolded, sliding her a sympathetic look.

Grace scowled at Jake. "Yes, hush," she added before turning back to Lexi. "I like your uncle fine, Lexi, but I'm not going to marry him. I'm just his therapist, and when he gets better, I'll leave and go help someone else."

Lexi's smiling face abruptly turned sour and her eyes filled with tears. "But I want you to stay!" She scrambled up from the table and ran across the room to the stairs, stomping up them as fast as her little feet could take her.

"Did I miss something?" Jake asked tiredly.

"That child is such a drama queen. She reminds me so much of—" Maura broke off with a frown as Jake muttered something under his breath.

Grace used the back of the couch to push herself to her feet. "I'll, uh, go talk to her."

Jake glanced her way. "She was crying awfully hard, Grace. Maybe you ought to let her calm down."

As if cued to the words, Lexi's wails rose in volume.

"Jake, it's just a temper tantrum," Maura argued firmly. "Every child has them occasionally, and Lex is no different." She looked at Grace. "Her room is the second on the right."

Grace nodded, conscious the couple spoke in low tones as she turned and made her way up the stairs. Outside Lexi's closed door, she knocked softly.

"Go away."

A smile pulled at Grace's mouth as she remembered those very words coming from Seth that morning. "I'm coming in," she murmured as she opened the door and gasped, unable to take in the explosion of soft, brilliant colors. Apparently Lexi had taken after her father, because she'd definitely left out a few details about her Aunt Arie liking to "paint."

The bedroom was gorgeous. Three of the walls were rolling hills of green grass, trees, flowers, mushroom houses, unicorns and tiny fairies with iridescent wings. Meandering here and there, up and down the walls, paths led to the fourth wall, where a castle was made all the more lifelike because of the roóm's peaked ceiling. A glance farther up had her mouth hanging open.

On one side of the ceiling more sparkling fairies played hide-and-seek in a sun-filled sky dotted with clouds. On the other half, the moon and stars glistened in the dark, swirling night, shining from the glitter in the paint.

Grace thought back to her own childhood bedroom. Pink walls and carpeting, sheer white curtains and a canopied bed. Her mother had tried to make their house into a home despite the yelling and flying fists. Tried to hide the abuse behind the picture-perfect facade.

A muffled sniffle drew Grace's attention. Lexi's head was buried in the mane of a stuffed unicorn that was bigger than she was.

"Lexi." Grace walked over to sit beside her on a satin comforter that matched the moat flowing around the castle walls. "Stop crying."

Lexi raised her face from the unicorn and glared at her. "Why?"

Grace crooked a finger at her. Lexi slowly pushed herself to her knees and crawled over to sit on Grace's lap. "Listen to me. I'm your uncle's therapist and nothing else. Yes, at one time, we dated because we liked each other, but that's over now. Soon your uncle Seth will be able to take care of himself and I'll have to leave."

"But why?"

After wiping a tear from Lexi's baby-soft cheek, Grace sighed. "Because I help people like your uncle. People who've been hurt and need me. It's my job and I like it very much."

"More than him?"

Grace faltered.

"Stay here 'n' do it," Lexi demanded before she had a chance to answer. The child batted her lashes coyly. "If you like us you will."

Grace chuckled warily at the stunt. Drama queen was right. "No, Lexi, I won't, and it has nothing to do with liking you. You may have your uncle and daddy wrapped around your finger, but those looks won't work with me. Now, are we clear? You know your uncle Seth and I are just…friends?"

Lexi looked disgruntled as she nodded. "'Kay, but that doesn't mean I can't wish it like in the wishing book at the lib'ry, right?"

"Lexi—"

The child grabbed hold of the necklace Grace wore around her neck. "Uncle Seff wants Daddy and Mommy to leave and take me with 'em, but they don't need me no more."

The knot in Grace's stomach grew. "They don't?"

"No. 'Cause of the baby. But if you get Uncle Seff better, I could stay here with him and keep him comp'ny."

Grace put a finger under Lexi's chin and raised her face so that the little girl met her gaze. "Lexi, your daddy and mommy wouldn't think of leaving you behind. You're their baby, too."

"But—"

"It would absolutely break their hearts to lose you even if they thought your uncle Seff would like it. Now, listen to me, okay? The baby won't ever replace you. After all, who's going to help your mommy take care of it if you're not with her?"

Lexi's brows pulled down into a fierce frown exactly like her father's—and uncle's. Grace pulled Lexi onto her knees on her lap so they were eye to eye. "So, would it be all right if I mentioned this worry of yours to your mom?"

Lexi was silent a long moment before she shyly tucked her face in the crook of Grace's neck and shrugged. "Uncle Seff *would* be all alone, but if you marry him—"

"No more talk about me marrying your uncle, remember? I mean it." She gently pushed Lexi away and pointed to the castle. "Before I forget, I want to tell you how much I like your room. It's beautiful."

"Aunt Arie painted it. Isn't she pretty?" Lexi pointed across the room.

Grace looked to where the child indicated and saw several framed photographs sitting atop a dresser. She spied one of Maura sitting next to someone who looked enough like her to pass as twins. But there was a uniqueness to Arie, a vibrancy and energy Maura just didn't have. Maura was the girl next door whereas Arie was…different. Spirited. Unusually striking.

"I like you, Grace."

Grace turned away from the photo, purposefully ending her curiosity over Seth's wife as she pulled the girl to her feet on the bed. "I like you, too. And now it's dinnertime. Want a piggyback ride downstairs?"

"Yeah!"

"And you'll remember what we've talked about?"

"Yes, ma'am."

Grace bit back a smile and helped Lexi climb onto her back, bouncing them out of the room with Lexi's giggles in her ear.

SETH LOOKED UP FROM the laptop computer Jake had loaned him and frowned when his brother entered his room without knocking.

He turned his attention back to the screen. "Why'd you do it, Jake?"

"Hire Grace?" Jake asked, scowling. "You wouldn't work with any of the others. What could it hurt?"

"I don't want her here."

"Grace is the least of your worries. Do us all a favor and cooperate."

Jake's cryptic comment drew Seth's gaze. "There a problem?"

Jake snorted and began pacing back and forth at the foot of his hospital bed. "Yeah, there's a problem. Phil Estes pointed out to me today that I'm a lawyer, not a rancher. You're going under, Seth, and I don't know what to do."

There was nothing Jake could do, and he didn't need his brother reminding him his livelihood suffered because of his lack of mobility. He'd made do before by working himself hard to make ends meet, but that wasn't possible now. All the hospital bills had taken a toll, and combined with the expense of Arie's funeral and the general maintenance of the ranch, he was about to lose the land passed down in his family for the past six generations.

He wouldn't sell, not even an acre, but if he had any chance of surviving at all he had to open his mind and consider the alternatives.

"You shouldn't have hired her," he said, going back to his original argument with Jake. "She's draining what little money I've got left."

Jake stomped across the room and snagged the straight-backed chair, flipping it around to straddle the seat and bracing his forearms over the back. "Seth, I know we've argued about your therapy before, but this is different. You don't want Grace here? Then pull yourself together. I can't support my family and this ranch indefinitely, and it's not fair that Maura graduated from cooking school only to give up her dream to stay here and play housekeeper for you."

"I never asked you to give anything up."

"You didn't have to ask, we're *family*. That's what family means, helping one another, supporting one another even during the worst of times. You did it with me and Maura, now it's our turn."

Seth laughed, softly at first, then loudly. "Since when are you in this chair with me?"

Jake's face darkened. "Seth—"

"I'm telling you to do what's best, Jake. Do what's right. Take Lexi and Maura and leave. Move to Helena, let Maura get settled, have the baby and then she can find a chef job in some fancy restaurant like she wants."

"And what about you? I'm supposed to leave you here? Like this?" Jake swept a hand out, indicating the wheelchair and the hospital bed, before shoving himself out of the chair. It toppled and landed on the floor with a carpet-muffled thud as Jake stalked across the room to the door. "You know, it's a good thing Dad can't see you. He put everything he had into this land, thinking you'd keep it safe."

"I can't walk!"

"No, you can't, can you? But every doc you've seen says you've got the potential to make a comeback and what do you do? You lie there and lord your disability over all our heads!"

Seth stared at Jake. "You think I *want* to be here?"

His brother slammed his fist against the wall. "No, I don't," he grated out. "But Maura's right. You can do more, you just won't. Your legs might not work, but your brain does and you won't even look at the ranch's paperwork while I'm bustin' my balls trying to make heads or tails of the stuff! You're lying here surfing the Net and feeling sorry for yourself while I'm *drowning!*" He hit the wall again.

"I put my life on hold, my career, my *marriage!* And for what? I'm thankful you helped us after Maura got pregnant. I'm thankful you took care of my child so that Maura and I could *both* finish school and have a decent life, but you— You're just sitting here! Instead, why don't you think of a way out of this mess? Stop being such a baby. Suck it up and deal with the hand God gave you!"

Jake yanked the door open and stalked out, and Seth grabbed the first thing that came to hand and threw it across the room. The plastic mug crashed into the wall and fell to the floor. The wake of silence was deafening, reminding him all too well of what was at stake. Jake was right. He *knew* Jake was right, but knowing it and doing something to save his livelihood from his hospital bed were two entirely different things. And though the doctors were hopeful, he still couldn't feel anything. The therapists had given up on him, walked away, so how could he not take that as a sign?

He scrubbed a hand over his face and groaned. His dad was probably looking down from heaven in bitter disappointment, and he couldn't blame him. Jake wasn't a rancher. His brother's heart and head had always been on the law, and he'd known when Jake and Maura changed their plans to help him after the accident, Jake wouldn't be able to keep things going.

The words on the computer screen blurred after staring at it for so long, but for every idea he'd come up with, he'd also thought of a logical reason to shoot it down. He'd run out of time and choices, and the only thing left to do was open his ranch to the public and hope for a reasonably quick return. But on what? What could he offer no one else did?

He hung his head low on his chest to stretch out the kinks and groaned aloud when his neck popped, easing the pressure and tension riding his shoulders. He'd tell Jake tomorrow after they'd both had a chance to cool off. See if he had any ideas on the matter. Maybe the fact he wasn't as oblivious as Jake seemed to think would help ease things between them.

GRACE HEARD JAKE STOMP out of Seth's room and finished drying the last of the supper dishes. Maura had taken Lexi up to read her a story before bedtime, so Grace had used the opportunity to clean up.

Jake's wife looked exhausted, and it was impossible to miss the strain between her and Jake. During her years as a physical therapist, she'd seen more than one marriage dissolve under the heavy weight of caring for an invalid, and Maura's pregnancy certainly couldn't be helping matters. Everyone knew how tired and emotional women got when they were pregnant, and the situation with Seth could only be adding to Maura's upset.

Grace searched until she found the correct cabinets and drawers for the bowls and utensils, the skillets and pans. Once everything was as neat as she could make it, she folded the towels before ambling down the hall to the home office.

"Don't bother knocking, just get in here."

Grace squared her shoulders and walked into the room, leaving the door open wide. "How did you know it was me?"

Jake sat back in the chair he occupied behind the large mahogany desk and laced his fingers behind his head. "It's Lexi's bedtime so Maura's upstairs. I'm sure she'll be down soon to play hostess, but as she's not seeking out my company much these days…I knew it had to be you."

"You guys are carrying a lot of responsibility that isn't yours." She dropped down into the seat opposite the time-scarred desk and watched as Jake closed his eyes with a grimace.

"Please tell me you had a fantastic day with him after I left. Lie to me."

"If you know I'd be lying, what's the point?"

His head lolled on his neck as he groaned. "He beats all I've ever seen. All he does is sit in that room and brood. We can't help him," Jake muttered, "not when he won't do anything to help himself."

Grace settled herself more comfortably on the padded leather seat and crossed her arms over her chest as she stared at her friend. "Recovery comes in stages, the first of which is wanting to fight to achieve it. And no matter how much a family might want it, the patient has to want it more. It's the way it works."

Jake grabbed a baseball from the credenza behind him and began rolling it between his hands. "Yeah, well, in the meantime he's killing my marriage."

"Don't let him. Whatever you do, don't let him destroy your life."

Jake groaned at her simplistic answer. "And just how am I supposed to keep it from happening? Maura's miserable and I can't blame her."

"Well, for what it's worth, I'm more than happy to babysit Lexi. Why don't you surprise Maura? Take her away from the ranch for a day out. Drive to Helena for dinner, maybe a little dancing. Romance her like the old days when you'd e-mail me and hit me up for ideas on what to do."

Jake looked stunned but quickly nodded. "We haven't done anything but work since the accident. She'd love that. You're sure you don't mind?"

"Not at all. Lexi's great. Although you might want to reassure her that the baby won't replace her."

"What?"

She laughed softly, her head tilted to one side as she filled him in.

Jake blinked, obviously dazed by the insight. "I had no—I'll talk to her. Have Maura talk to her, too. Play up the whole big-sister role."

"I'm sure she'll like that."

Jake frowned. "Did she say anything else?"

Releasing a sigh, she shrugged. "She doesn't understand why Seth won't play with her like he used to, but that's normal, too. A lot of children blame themselves for things that happen to the adults around them. I'm not a parent so I can only tell you what I know from psychology classes and experiences with my patients, but I think reassuring her that she's still your baby girl will go a long way."

Jake nodded, his expression sad. "It's been so crazy around here, she's definitely gotten pushed to the side in the shuffle. God, what a mess." He rubbed his eyes as though trying to wipe away the weariness. "Okay…we'll take care of Lex. So what about you?"

Taken aback at the sudden change in topic, she hesitated. "What about me?" She didn't like the look on his face. Before her eyes, Jake transformed from concerned dad to concerned friend in a split second.

"I know we've only talked sporadically over the years, but you want to tell me how you're holding up coming back here and facing Seth."

Nothing like getting straight to the point. She licked her lips and tried to formulate an answer he might accept. "I'm fine."

Jake snorted. "Here's a tip, Grace—whenever my clients get defensive, I know something's up."

"I'm not defensive, I'm…tired. It's been a trying day." She played with the hem of her long T-shirt. "It was such a surprise to see Seth in the condition he's in."

"He's needed you long before now."

Guilt surged, reminding her how many times Jake had asked her to come help Seth. She'd used every excuse under the sun to avoid the prospect, delaying the inevitable as long as possible. "Play nice now. It didn't help you hadn't told him I'd agreed to be his new therapist," she complained.

"Shock value?"

She wrinkled her nose at Jake's attempt at humor. "More like you avoided the battle," she countered. "The good news is I've worked with more serious injuries than Seth's and had some success. However, I don't think I need to tell you his attitude is his worst enemy." Shoving herself up from the chair, she walked over to a wall lined with books ranging from Montana history to art. She fingered a gold-embossed spine.

Behind her, Jake's chair squeaked. "Things will blow over soon enough. You and Seth were close once. You can be again."

Groaning, she glared at him over her shoulder. "Jake, don't you start, too. There's nothing left and even if there were—" she held up a hand "—it wouldn't matter. It's over."

Jake's expression was solemn. "Sorry. Guess I'd hoped that maybe you two could work through things."

"We can't."

"You guys argued, but I've never understood why you took things to the extreme you did." She didn't respond, and after a moment, Jake shrugged. "Okay, fine, new subject. The, uh, docs say they think Seth can make a full recovery."

"I agree," she murmured, now that they were on a safer ground.

"So even though he's been difficult, you'll stick with him?"

She nodded, fingering Seth's name inscribed on one of the large belt buckles on display in front of her. Seth had won numerous competitions before his father had died, before taking over the ranch and leaving behind his carefree days for a more stable existence. But she remembered seeing him at a rodeo once, his cowboy swagger intact as he won the prize. Tall and broad-shouldered, his short dark hair covered by his cowboy hat and oh, his eyes.

Shaking off the memories, Grace moved on down the row of bookshelves, lingering over a picture of a toothless Lexi, before finding herself in front of the window staring out at the darkened landscape.

Maura cleared her throat from the doorway. "Lexi's asleep and I brought coffee. Decaf. Anyone up for a cup?"

Grace nodded as she raised a brow at Jake, silently asking if he wanted her to broach the subject of Lexi and her fears. Jake nodded imperceptibly as Maura poured them coffee and the three of them settled in for a chat.

CHAPTER FIVE

"GOOD MORNING, SLEEPYHEAD. Time to rise and shine." Grace clapped her hands and watched as Seth opened one eye but just as quickly shut it again, a foul word escaping him.

She laughed. Of all the ways she would've expected Seth to act, this wasn't what she'd imagined. Seth had always been so easygoing. Friendly and flirtatious. Tall, dark and handsome in every sense. Now, well—tall, dark and grumpy didn't have quite the same effect.

"Time for therapy."

"I told you yesterday I'm not going."

"Poor baby, not enough grouchy sleep?"

Both eyes flickered open at her taunt. "Are you always this irritating?"

Another laugh bubbled up before she could squelch it. He really did look fierce and she knew his expression ought to bother her more than it did. "'Fraid so. I'm an early bird."

He snagged his pillow and put it over his face. "I'm not. Not anymore."

"Come on," she chided cheerfully. "Jake had to drive in and take care of some things at his office, so if you're wanting him to help you out of bed to the bathroom you're out of luck. I'm it." She pulled the pillow off his head and they wound up in a tug-of-war to see who'd keep possession.

She won.

Seth cursed long and loud.

"Gotta get stronger if you're going to toss me out, you know." He told her where to go and she wagged a finger at him. "Now, what kind of language is that for a grown man to use? What if Lexi heard you? You want that coming out of her sweet little mouth?"

"Grace—"

She smiled. "Correct me if I'm wrong, but aren't most ranchers up before dawn?" she asked as she tossed the pillow behind her. She reached out to grab his covers next.

Seth slammed a hand down on top of both of hers to hold them where they were. "I don't want to get up."

Her brows rose, and even though her heart kicked up several beats, she didn't back down. This time with him was critical. She had to set the boundaries. Make sure he knew how far she'd go to help him. Despite the fear eating away at her confidence, she squared her shoulders and plunged in with both feet.

"You can't stay in bed all day," she said, pulling.

He drew in a sharp breath. "Let *go*."

She tugged again and all of a sudden she realized why he didn't want to get up—

He already was.

Grace released the blanket as her face burned with heat. "Oh, uh, y-your chair. How could I have forgotten to get your chair?"

Seth's chair wasn't but a few inches away from the bed, but for all the effort she put into positioning it, repositioning it and making sure the supports were at the right height, one would've thought she'd never seen a wheelchair before in her life.

"Be th-thinking about what you want to get out of our session today," she murmured when she finally worked up the courage to face him again.

"I'm not going to therapy." But in one quick motion Seth threw the covers off his waist and legs with a look that dared her to say a word about his…problem. "You can help me out of bed. But that's it."

Grace hesitated—who wouldn't given the situation?—then moved into position and locked her hands beneath his arms. "On three." She counted off the numbers, transferred Seth to his wheelchair and placed his feet in the supports. All without a word from him. Or *to him,* considering she still couldn't look at him.

Finally the silence got to her. She was an adult. She was a professional. *That* happened.

And just because it was Seth, well—

"You're not doing yourself any good sitting in your chair or lying in bed all day. You have to move around, be as active as you can so that your muscles and nerves get working again. And you need to keep your upper body strong. You should be getting yourself in and out of bed without assistance."

"You don't want to do it?" he drawled, not bothering to disguise his intent. "Leave."

Not for the first time she wished she could. Usually she traveled from patient to patient, with little downtime in between. She'd lived briefly in California, Ohio, New York, Tennessee and, lastly, North Carolina. If she had a break between clients, she tried to do something fun, sort of like a minivacation to unwind. But as she'd only just taken on Seth's case, she didn't have another client lined up yet and—

She wasn't quitting.

Grace swung Seth's chair around to face the bathroom and grabbed a fresh pair of flannel drawstring pajama pants and a T-shirt from atop his dresser where she'd lain them before waking him up. Without comment she dropped them onto his lap and then rolled him through the bathroom door.

"Let's get you showered."

SETH SEETHED AT HER WORDS. Jake or whatever *male* therapist present usually helped him remove his pants before transferring him to the seat lining his specially equipped stall, but no way was he going to let Grace perform that chore.

"I'll do it."

"Can you?"

He grabbed the wheels of his chair so she couldn't move him any farther. "Get out."

He'd stopped wearing underwear after the accident. All he had to do was lift himself up and shuck his bottoms.

But that wasn't easy to do when he couldn't use his legs for balance, and he didn't have a third hand to pull his pants down. Where was Jake? Had he left without helping to get back at him for their argument?

"Fine. Shower. I'll be back in a little while with breakfast and we'll discuss your therapy."

"I'm not going to therapy!"

Grace ignored his bellow and shut the bathroom door with an annoyingly soft *click*.

Seth cursed and slapped his fist down on the armrest of his chair, swearing again when pain streaked up his arm. Stubborn woman. She'd probably stand outside until he was in the shower, waiting to find an excuse to barge in so she could humiliate him.

He glared at the door and then reached back to turn the lock. A grunt escaped him as he dragged his shirt over his head, ignoring the hamper near the sink and letting it drop to the floor. She wanted something to do? Grace could pick up after him, at least that would give Maura a break.

The drawstring of his pants hung in his lap in a loose knot. He freed the strings and shoved, tossing his upper body from side to side in the chair, inching the cotton pants down. He had to stop and rest twice, but he finally got the material out from under his butt, wondering more than once why God had bothered to keep him alive.

He shoved the pants down his legs and yanked them off his feet, sweat dripping off the tip of his nose. His arms shook, his whole body was hot. Even his legs. He leaned back in his chair, out of breath now that the task was finally completed, then groaned as he spied the clock on the wall.

It had taken him seven minutes to get his freakin' pants off.

OUTSIDE THE BATHROOM Grace watched the clock on Seth's bedside table, counting the minutes and listening closely as Seth cursed and grumbled and struggled to free himself from his clothing. Finally she heard the shower door rumbling as it slid open and closed.

Relieved that he'd finally managed, she glanced around the room and froze at the sight of Seth's rumpled bed. The sheet he'd held on to with such a death grip hung over the side, and despite her will to the contrary, her face heated.

Moaning, she closed her eyes and shook her head. How embarrassing. For them both. But not unusual, and although in some cases impotence was a problem, maybe it wouldn't be for Seth. She hoped not, but only time would tell. Spinal injuries in men could take on a number of facets, one of which was the ability to have an erection, but not the ability to maintain one.

Regardless, that was a subject she wasn't about to broach with Seth anytime soon, not if she could help it.

Noting the time, she left his room. In the kitchen, Maura gave her a sympathetic smile but didn't comment on Seth's shouting, and the woman's red-rimmed eyes said all too clearly her morning hadn't gone well, either. In surprisingly easy silence they prepared two breakfast trays, and Grace lifted one with a murmur of thanks and carried it down the hall past Seth's room. She put that tray on the card table she'd already prepared in the gym and went back for the second.

As she entered the kitchen, Grace broke the silence. "Maura, you, uh, might want to take your breakfast upstairs and hang out a bit when Lexi wakes up. You know, keep her out of earshot."

Maura laughed softly, the sound sad. "Going to be that bad, huh?"

Grace shrugged, careful to keep the second tray balanced. "Maybe. I honestly never know what's going to happen."

Maura tilted her head to the side, unable to hide the tears welling in her eyes. "If he would just try," she whispered, her hands braced on the counter. "I keep reminding myself of how much he's helped us, but we helped ourselves, too, you know? Why won't he?"

Grace tried to think of something to lighten the mood. "He'll get there. If it's any consolation I've had worse patients."

"Really?"

She nodded, relating several quick stories about the patients she'd encountered who'd cursed her, smacked her and even spit on her. Her anecdotes did the trick and pretty soon Maura was laughing, albeit in resignation.

"So I guess Seth isn't as bad as he could be, then?"

Grace offered the younger woman a smile. "Nope. Be patient a bit longer. Maybe we'll get through to him soon."

Maura's gaze hardened. "I hope so. I honestly

don't know how much more of this I can take."
Tears appeared once again and she turned away,
busying herself with getting a small plastic plate
from the dishwasher.

"I've got to get back. We'll talk later, okay?"

Maura nodded, obviously unable to speak.

Grace pushed Maura's upset to the back of her
mind as she turned and carried the second tray down
the hall, leaving it on the hall table outside Seth's
door where it could be seen—and hopefully
smelled—from within his bedroom.

That done, she reentered Seth's room and then positioned herself outside his bathroom. She heard the
shower shut off and her nerves kicked into overdrive.

She didn't like these types of encounters. Never
had and never would. Seth's mutterings from within
the bathroom didn't help, either, because with each
one she could hear his anger building as he tried to
perform the simplest of tasks, things he used to do
without conscious thought.

The door to the bathroom opened and swung toward her. Grace caught the paneled wood before it
hit her in the face, and made sure it blocked her presence from Seth's line of vision. A moment later he
emerged, his T-shirt sticking to his back and shoulders where he hadn't dried himself completely.

As though right on cue, he lifted his head, his
shoulders and back taut as he noted the open door

and heavenly scent of Maura's home-cooked breakfast wafting in from the hallway.

Eggs and bacon, biscuits and sausage gravy. Orange juice and fresh brewed coffee, strong and black the way Seth liked it.

Grace's mouth watered thinking about how good everything would taste and her stomach growled loudly. Eyes wide, she clamped a hand over her belly and waited anxiously to see if she'd tipped Seth off to her presence behind him.

He hadn't heard her. But only because he was too busy cursing, having realized he was going to have to get his breakfast himself by venturing *outside* his room—which she'd learned over dinner last night was something he hadn't done since his last therapist left. He ate here, slept here. Brooded here. But all that was about to change.

Go on. Go get it, for pity's sake.

Seth's reluctance was obvious as he wheeled himself to the doorway of his bedroom and leaned forward to peer into the hall. He scowled, but a second later he crossed the threshold, his wheelchair more out than in, and she grinned.

Gotcha.

She raced across the floor on silent feet, shoved his wheelchair the few inches it took to get it completely out into the hall, slammed the door and locked it behind her.

"What the—" Seth turned, his already thunderous expression darkening even more. *"Open the door!"*

She shook her head. "No."

Seth grabbed the wheels of his chair and awkwardly swung himself around, the supports under his feet threatening to clip her ankles. "Get out of my way."

Raising her hands, Grace stepped to the side. *Three, two, one.*

A savage curse split the air. "You *locked* it? Where's the key? Give it to me."

She leaned against the wall in a pose as casual as she could make it and shook her head again. "Nope."

Seth's dark eyes narrowed into slits. "Is that all you can say?" he demanded. "You locked me out of my room—*in my own house*—and that's all you can *say?*"

Her gaze slid to the tray. "Your food's getting cold."

More curses filled the air, and Grace sincerely hoped Maura had heeded her advice and gone upstairs to keep an eye on Lexi.

"Open the door and I'll eat it!"

"Nope." She grabbed the tray, careful to stay out of arm's reach just in case. "Come on into the gym."

Seth laughed, the sound cold, deceitful in its softness. "Why? You get your thrills out of cripples?"

She froze, completely unable to move or voice a protest.

Seth had managed to knock the wind from her. Made her want to curl up into a protective ball. The lash of his words was as brutal as her stepfather's fists. What she and Seth had shared was special to her, memorable. Tender and sweet.

Yes, Seth had wanted more, but all the times she'd stopped him, kept him from going further, she'd thought he'd understood. Thought he'd respected her decision to wait since they hadn't known each other all that long.

Now he was taunting her with it?

She lifted her chin high before putting one foot in front of the other until she reached the relative safety of the gym. All without saying a word. Not that she could have.

How could she have been so naive? Seth was a man. Five years older than herself, and twenty-two to her seventeen when they'd dated.

Seth's griping rang loud and long throughout the hall as she set the tray on the wobbly card table. Unbalanced herself, she sat, dazed at how much Seth's words had hurt her.

Long minutes passed before she heard the push-whirl of Seth's wheelchair. She wanted nothing more than to jump to her feet and get out of there, but if she didn't stay and face him now, how would she ever find the courage?

Seth rolled to a stop inside the doorway, staring

her down for a long, breathless moment before his gaze settled on the two trays in front of her. Jaw locked, he focused on the tray opposite her as he rolled himself across the room.

"Hungry?" she asked, her voice coming out husky and drawn, more like a croak and lacking the strength she wanted.

Seth wheeled himself close to the table and ignored her, picking up his fork to shovel a bite into his mouth. The tension between them mounted, filled the air and grew until she was so tense her spine felt like it would snap from the pressure.

Snarling, he pointed the fork at her with a jab. "If you ever do something like that again, I'm going to—"

"What?" she dared softly, proud of herself when her voice strengthened at last.

His features darkened beneath the shaggy beard. "Grace, don't do this. You don't want me angry at you and I don't like being tricked. I didn't like it then and I sure as hell don't like it now. Get out of my house and leave me alone."

"I can't. And for the record, I don't like being cursed at or accused of things I haven't done. I never tricked you."

Seth's gaze stole her breath as she witnessed the turbulent emotions flashing in his eyes.

After a moment, after neither of them moved,

Seth seemed to come to a decision, his anger banked behind a mask of indifference. "So now what?"

Grace lowered her hands to her lap and grabbed her paper napkin, slowly and methodically ripping it to shreds beneath the table where he couldn't see. "Now we eat. Then we work together to make you better. I've gone over your file, Seth. The potential you have for a full recovery is good. Better than good, it's wonderful, but only if you can pull yourself out of this—this mood and use all that anger and frustration to your benefit."

Seth turned his full attention to the meal in front of him, ignoring her words, ignoring her. Grace watched in amazement as he finished the food off in a minimal amount of bites, wiped his mouth and wheeled himself away from her, toward one of the two windows facing the backyard.

All appetite gone, she shoved her food away and wrapped her hands around her coffee mug to warm them. "I know you're mad about being locked out and I'm sorry about that, but I'd like you to understand why I did it. It isn't often I have a patient so determined *not* to get better, I have to resort to these types of measures. Now, since you're awake and showered and *here*," she continued, "why not make the most of it? Let me give you a therapy session."

"You may have tricked me out of my room but you didn't win, Grace. I haven't agreed to anything."

"This isn't a game, but the only person who'll lose at this is you. Surely you see that?"

"I said no."

She squeezed the mug. She'd pushed him hard today, very hard considering he'd had to accept her help to get out of bed, gotten locked out of his room and forced to the gym. *Baby steps.*

"Come back over here and finish your coffee. Tell me about your ranch and all the changes you've made in the past ten years," she offered, quickly giving him an alternative to ease the sting of his first refusal. What had she expected? A miracle on the second day?

"Why?"

"I'm interested," she murmured, shrugging. "The addition to the house is beautiful. You…you did a good job making it all blend."

Seth didn't acknowledge her words, and gathering her courage, she turned and found herself staring into his eyes.

Grace realized in that moment that all of her patients had the same look. Older, younger, men, women, children. In the beginning they all stared at her as though searching to find something within her that they couldn't find within themselves. Strength? Determination? Maybe. She wasn't sure. All she knew was that it required her to come up with a variety of ways to get them to open up and cooperate. Seth was simply making her do the same.

Turning back to the table, she fiddled with her shredded napkin, then settled herself more comfortably in the uncomfortable chair and waited, hoping her pose was that of patience.

Minutes passed.

"You ever have a patient like me?"

"Stubborn? Oh, yeah."

"I meant the same injury. Did they walk again?"

She wanted to give him the answer he craved, but couldn't. She wouldn't lie. Especially not to Seth. "No. Not exactly. Every case is different, but I promise you I will do my best to help you. If you let me."

She glanced at him again, hurting inside when she glimpsed the despair in Seth's eyes. "Tell me about the ranch," she urged again.

"Why?"

"Want to have your door unlocked anytime soon?"

The anger returned to his gaze, outshining the desperation. "That's blackmail."

She laughed softly. "That it is—so deal with it. Tell me about the ranch, or spend the day in here with me."

Seth began talking.

CHAPTER SIX

"YOU, UH, WOULDN'T BE READY for a walk, would you?"

Grace looked up as she stacked the last of her and Seth's dirty breakfast dishes, more than a little pleased with how things had turned out. Although reluctant, he'd returned to the table, drunk his coffee and filled her in on ten years of ranching. All in all, the morning had gone well.

"Everything okay?"

Maura laughed, her gaze lowered. "Not really. Even though I was upstairs, I still managed to hear Seth hollering. I thought we could both use a break."

Grace chuckled. "Got that right. That man has a great affinity for hiding out in his room."

"He's pretty much been there since Jake brought him home from the hospital. He gets angrier and angrier as the days go by."

Grace lifted the trays loaded with dishes and followed Maura to the kitchen. Neither of them spoke as they passed Seth's room.

While they placed the dishes in the dishwasher, Maura explained that Lexi had been picked up by a friend and taken to town for reading hour at the library.

"So we've got about an hour and a half. Maybe two if Meghan's mom has a few errands to run. Want to get out of here before the walls close in on us?"

Despite the fatigue pulling at her from her sleepless night, one glance into Maura's anxious features wouldn't let her say no. Maybe the walk would do her good. Clear her head and help her relax. She nodded and the two of them made their way through the house to their coats hanging by the back door.

Outside the air was brisk, causing the corn stalks by the porch steps to rustle in the breeze. In the distance snow clouds layered the mountaintops and she shivered at the sight. Winters in Montana were hard and long. But instead of memories filled with snowball fights and sledding, she remembered being stuck in the house with a drunk. Scuttling out of the way as quickly as possible so as not to draw her stepfather's attention.

"I don't know how you do it," Maura said as they headed away from the house and down the driveway. "Jake acts like it's no big deal taking care of Seth and so do you, but I feel taken advantage of sometimes. Not all the time, but sometimes. How do you *not* feel that way?"

Grace shrugged, shoving her hands inside her pockets for warmth. "Well, for one it's my job so I'm used to the way things work. I also lack the personal attachment you and Jake have to Seth, so that helps, too."

"But you do have a personal connection to Seth," Maura argued. "Jake said you two were *really* close once. Please stop my ranting at any time, but after seeing you with Seth yesterday and hearing the fight this morning, there's something about you that makes me think you aren't as cool as you let on where he's concerned."

Grace attempted a smile. "Very perceptive of you." She inhaled and sighed. "Okay, I admit it, he gets to me, too."

Just then she caught Roy Bernard eyeing them from within the open doors of the barn. Maura didn't seem to notice the man, so she pretended she didn't, either. They left the grassy area near the house and began walking down the long driveway, a chill raking over her as Bernard continued to stare.

Maura shot her a look. "Jake and I seem to be fighting all the time now. I hate it. It's not what I want considering I'm getting ready to give birth."

She nodded, sympathetic. No woman would want tension and chaos before bringing home a second child.

"But to be here willing and able to help, and Seth

so *un*willing to help himself! Grace, I turned down the job of my dreams at the best restaurant in Montana. And Jake—a few months back he turned down a partnership because he knew he couldn't handle the load. I can't even decorate a room for the baby because the house isn't ours. Not that there's money to do that now, anyway, with Jake's paycheck keeping the ranch afloat."

With every item Maura listed her strides increased, and for a woman who waddled when she walked, Grace was amused to note Maura waddled pretty quickly.

"So what would you like Jake to do?"

Tears filled Maura's eyes and she dashed them away with her fingers. "That's just it—I don't *know!* We can't leave Seth. I *know* that, and I don't want to. Honestly, I don't. He's family and he needs us. And there's Lexi. That child loves him so much. She doesn't want to move at all. I know she hears us fighting, so it's understandable she's confused." More tears trickled down Maura's cheeks. "What you said last night— She thinks I don't *want* her?"

"Maura, I'm sure she was exaggerating her fears," Grace soothed. "She simply needs to hear you and Jake say out loud that she isn't going to be replaced. That's all."

Maura nodded but looked unconvinced. "Maybe. I told her last night and again this morning. She can't handle any more upset in her life especially after losing Arie. She was young, but she remembers Arie fairly well and feels the loss. Arie was her prime caregiver for two whole years and they were close. And now Seth—*oooh!* Doesn't he *see* what he's doing to her? Does he care? *No!*"

Maura turned, her footsteps slowing to a halt on the gravel and dirt. "I love how you stand up to him, Grace. Do you have any idea how much I want to go and scream at him for acting the way he is?" She laughed bitterly "Like that would help, yelling at a man who can't walk."

Grace stopped about a foot away from Jake's wife, her head tilted to one side. "Maura, if you want to yell, yell. Don't feel sorry for him. Pitying Seth isn't what he needs."

"But how can I not pity him? Oh, God, I feel so *guilty!*"

"For stating the truth?" she pointed out. "Don't. Guilt is normal, as is anger. You've every right to be angry and upset when you've given up so much to help Seth and he behaves the way he does."

Maura turned and began walking again, away from the driveway to a worn path that led to a stand of tall pines. In the distance Grace heard the sound of water.

"So it's normal," Maura muttered. "So what? It doesn't change anything."

No, it didn't. Following her, Grace watched her footing and tried to think of something that would bolster the other woman's feelings. "We'll work together. Get Seth to realize what he's missing. Help him cope. And even yell back at him when he yells at us. Sometimes the most stoic patients have to be made to feel again. They're boiling inside because they have too many emotions to handle so they shut down entirely to escape."

Maura was silent a moment. "When I met Seth for the first time, he gave me the biggest hug and kiss, all to tease Jake. But now Seth is—" she closed her eyes "—a royal pain in the butt!"

Grace laughed. "Agreed."

They stepped into a clearing, the water she'd heard earlier turning out to be a fast-moving creek about a foot wide. On the other side was a cabin.

"That's Arie's studio," Maura informed her. "That's what Jake and I fought over this morning. I come here when I absolutely have to get out of the house and want to be alone. There's a bed up in the loft, a small kitchen. We could build onto the living room and add a full bath if we got all of Arie's things out of the way like I—"

Maura broke off and Grace pulled her gaze away from the picturesque little cabin to stare at her. Why hadn't she realized? Of course Maura wanted a home of her own. She couldn't blame her. But she also didn't want to involve herself in Jake and Maura's marriage to any great extent. Listening was one thing, but how could she offer any concrete advice about something she'd never experienced?

"It's close to the house. I mean, look how quickly we walked here. Minutes, that's all." She shook her head. "I asked Jake to talk to Seth. After Arie died, none of us could handle coming here. It was too hard."

"I'd...I'd forgotten she was your sister."

Maura butted the toe of her shoe against a rock. "We didn't get along growing up. Not at all." She turned to look at Grace, her expression sad. "I was younger than Arie, born after my mom and her dad got together. Arie always thought they favored me because of it."

"I think most siblings feel that way at some time or another."

"Maybe. But once Arie started seeing Seth, well, it was different. We finally found some common ground loving two brothers. For the first time, it was nice having a sister."

Grace followed Maura as she walked slowly along the side of the creek. It hurt like crazy to think of Seth with someone else, but—

"Jake and I were engaged and we were planning to marry once he graduated, but when I got pregnant that speeded things up. Jake probably told you we both talked about dropping out."

"Yeah." That much she knew. When she and Seth broke up, Jake had agreed not to discuss Seth. Still, every now and then Jake would slip and she relished the tidbits of information he'd pass along.

Maura nodded, a sad smile curling her lips. "Silly, I know, but we couldn't think beyond the next nine months. Then Seth came charging up to campus one weekend because he knew something was going on. He and Arie met and hit it off and then somehow we all wound up married and under the same roof. It was kind of scary, how fast it all happened."

"I'm sorry for your loss."

"Arie was speeding." Maura bent and picked up a small stone, tossing it into the water where it landed with a *plop*. "I was farther along when Arie found out she was pregnant, but it was so much fun. We laughed over body changes and moods, cravings—until she miscarried." Her head lifted, her gaze fixated on the cabin. "She wasn't the same after that. She and Seth fought a lot, but we managed to stay close, which was great. The only thing Arie seemed to enjoy was Lexi. She loved her. Painted pictures for her and of her."

"Lexi's room is gorgeous."

Maura picked up another rock and ran her thumb over its smooth surface. "She finished it just before she died." Maura swept a hand toward the cabin.

"Enough time has passed now, and if we're going to stay in North Star, I want us to move in here, but Jake won't even consider it." Maura glanced at her, the tip of her nose red from the cold and her tears.

Not sure what to say, Grace studied the cabin closely. "It's beautiful. And it would be a wonderful home."

Maura's face reflected her misery as she nodded, then turned and began walking away from the cabin instead of toward it, her shoulders hunched, head down.

Grace wanted to call her back to ask to see the inside and listen as Maura rattled on about Seth's wife and the changes she'd like to make to the cabin, but she quickly reminded herself about curiosity killing the cat. It was none of her business, and her motives weren't exactly aboveboard. It hurt to think of Seth married to someone else. Sleeping with her, caring for her. *Loving* her.

But considering the way she'd left him, knowing what he was about to ask, and knowing she couldn't give him what he wanted, she couldn't be jealous or upset that he'd fallen in love with someone else. She certainly couldn't blame him, especially given the time that had lapsed in between their breakup and his marriage to Arie. He hadn't gone out and immediately found someone else. No, he'd waited, fallen in love with a woman totally her opposite.

DURING THE NEXT WEEK and a half Seth spent a lot of time talking. He had to, in an attempt to satisfy Grace's demands so he could return to his room. She entered his room not long after dawn and bullied him into getting up. That done, next was the fight over breakfast and whether or not he was going to get any. As on the day she'd locked him out of his bedroom, if he wanted to eat, he had to follow her into the gym, where it had become a custom for them to breakfast together. A custom they'd fallen into after he'd refused her orders and wound up not getting any food as a result. None.

He'd made it until late afternoon before he'd gotten over his rage and unlocked the door to his room. Sure enough, right outside was a covered tray waiting for him. But to get it he had to go out into the hall where Grace waited to shanghai him.

He chuckled. Whether he liked it or not, Grace's unorthodox methods intrigued him as did her determination to help him. She kept coming back. Morning after morning. No matter what he said to her. No matter how loud he cursed or how quiet he got. No matter the games or challenges she had to throw out in order to get him to cooperate. She never gave up. Which made him more than a little bit ashamed of his behavior.

Now here he was, drawn to Grace with her full,

smiling mouth and mysterious eyes. He'd never met another woman so bossy, so irritating, so determined or so tempting in all his life.

"Go on," Grace urged. "You were saying?"

Seth stared at her blankly, unable to remember what he'd been saying before his thoughts had taken off on a tangent of their own.

Grace was easy to talk to and he'd made a fool of himself, rambling on about the ranch, Lexi, his months at rehab and expounding on his and Jake's childhood adventures. She'd even asked him about Arie, but that was one subject he refused to discuss with his ex-girlfriend. Regardless, Grace seemed genuinely interested in what he had to say. And she wouldn't let him return to his room otherwise.

The problem was, she never opened up to him, never said anything about the past or why she'd left. They discussed casual things, unimportant things, and with every word said between them that didn't delve into their breakup and the questions remaining, the tension between them escalated.

As did her nightmares.

Every night while he lay awake staring up at the ceiling, torn between losing his land and thinking of Grace, she cried out in her sleep in the room next to his. Leading him to believe something or someone had hurt her, put the shadows under her eyes and created the wary expression she wore when she wasn't aware she was being watched. There was a sadness about her, something he was only just realizing she'd always had, even while they'd dated.

"Seth? Hey, you in there?"

He picked up a cold strip of bacon and began eating it to keep from having to admit he'd forgotten their topic of conversation. Grace raised a brow as seconds ticked by and the silence stretched between them. She didn't press him, though.

No, he could sit there and glare at her and she didn't seem to mind. Because whether they talked or not, he had to answer her questions or else he couldn't go back to his room. And if he tried to before she was ready to let him?

His face heated at the memory of trying to beat her to the door and losing. Badly.

She played dirty and gloated when she won.

No, his mind corrected, secretly relishing the backbone and spunk Grace revealed on a daily basis. She played to win, and like it or not, he admired that about her.

Grace didn't pity him and she gave as good as she got. She wasn't uncomfortable around his wheelchair, which was quite a switch from Maura and Jake falling all over themselves trying to help him. Did he need anything? Was he hungry? Thirsty? Hot? Cold? Did he want something to read?

Grace sat back and told him to do it, get it, fix it himself.

Once upon a time, he'd have done the same, said the same thing to a person sitting back and letting the world pass them by. Had the accident changed him that much?

The thought staggered him.

"Come on, quit brooding. I can see your mind whirling and it can't be good."

"I'm not brooding," he shot back automatically, even though they both knew it was a lie. "I was wondering what it's going to be today. How're you going to try to pressure me into therapy this time? You haven't dumped me on the floor and tried to work on me regardless."

There was a hint of a smile on her lush mouth. "Sounds like you know that tactic from experience. What were the results?"

He grinned in satisfaction. "He had a black eye and bloodied mouth. Not that I'd ever hit a woman," he corrected when he saw her shoot him a disturbed glance. "You've got nothing to worry about there, Grace, and you know it. With you, I'd just have to think of another way to…distract you."

Her gaze avoided his as a blush rose into her cheeks. "That, uh, tactic does work at times, but with you? Uh-uh. Not a good idea on the part of whichever therapist tried it. All things considered,

I decided a little while longer without therapy won't hurt if it means you'll come to terms with the fact I'm not leaving. Besides, I get paid either way, so you're the one wasting your money by not taking advantage of my help," she added, her voice chiding, but throaty and appealing to the man in him.

Throaty? Appealing? He would be crazy to go there again.

"It's a simple strategy but an effective one, I think," she murmured, her eyes twinkling. "You're worried about the financial burden of my pay on the ranch, so the best way of getting rid of me is to co-operate, get better, and then I can leave. See? Easy."

She was trying to wear him down again, this time using his strapped-for-cash logic against him, and if he were honest, he'd admit it was working. He'd given her his worst and she still hadn't budged, making him wonder what could it hurt to try her therapy. After a while, when he *still* hadn't made any progress, maybe she'd be like the others, admit he was a lost cause, and leave. But by then he'd be out of cash as well and what good would that do him?

"Does your question mean you're finally ready to bite the bullet and let me help you?" she continued, her tone a tad hopeful.

Seth picked up his coffee cup and raised it to his lips to drink the last of it with one long swallow, studying her over the rim. "Nope," he countered, deliberately using her favorite response to him.

At first he'd wondered how she spent the rest of her day when he closed himself off in his room, but then he usually saw her and Maura and Lexi outside his windows. And every now and again he'd crack one of the windows open to eavesdrop on their conversations. Whatever it took to pass the time.

That's how he knew Grace and Maura were plotting. And that it was only a matter of time before Grace broached the subject with him that had Maura so upset with Jake.

"Okay, then, how about that arm wrestling rematch today? Think you're up to beating me yet?"

He pretended to consider it a moment, then shook his head with a slight grin. "Not arm wrestling."

No, he wasn't going to tip his hand just yet. The good food and healthy appetite had definitely made a difference in him, but until he could challenge Grace at arm wrestling and win the prize teasing the back of his mind, he'd hold out.

Grace wrinkled her nose at him and plucked the napkin from her lap to toss it onto her plate. "Well, fine, if you're not going to cooperate I'll go find Lexi and give Maura a chance to relax." She hesitated. "Want to join us?"

His smile faded and he glared at her for tempting him with something he wanted so badly. "No."

His mood darkened even more at the thought of being stuck within the same four walls he'd stared at for the past six months, but he wouldn't accept her invitation. He didn't want to sit back and watch them. He wanted to ride alongside his niece, chase her through the garden to the tree house he'd built for her in back. Show Grace his ranch and talk about all the things he hadn't had a chance to do yet.

Not being able to do any of that emasculated him.

"You've done well today." She glanced at her watch. "You finished your breakfast over two hours ago and you didn't try to take off like your chair was on fire."

He grunted in response, frowning when he saw his mug was empty. Maybe he'd have another cup. After all, when he went back to his room it was getting harder and harder to stay there and be satisfied with the television and computer and books.

"If you change your mind about going outside—"

"I won't."

She looked disappointed. Should he go? He could sit on the porch. Get some fresh air. It'd certainly be good to get out and breathe. Stare at the mountains and dream about better days.

"Have fun, then. I know we will." Grace got up from the table, stacked their dishes and trays on top of one another and picked them up to leave. "The jack-o'-lantern Lexi wants me to help her make should last until Halloween, don't you think?"

He nodded reluctantly. Helping Lex carve a jack-o'-lantern had always been his job.

"Well, if you change your mind, we'll be scraping out a pumpkin on the back porch."

SETH GLANCED AT THE CLOCK and scowled. He was going to lose what little sanity he had left if he stayed in his room any longer. He'd watched enough television to last him a lifetime, a fact proved when his favorite western couldn't hold his attention.

Outside the window he saw Hank toss a bridle aside in disgust. Bridles and harnesses, all the tack on the ranch, had to be cleaned and repaired, but with everyone busy, the equipment was in sorry shape—just like its owner.

He leaned forward, his heart pounding. Fixing the tack would break his boredom. Give him something to do and help out at the same time.

He rapped loudly on the window with his knuckles, gained Hank's attention, and then opened the window wide.

Hank jogged the distance as fast as his bowed legs could carry him. "Need help, Seth?"

The only time he and Hank had been face-to-face since he'd returned home from the rehab hospital had been when he'd fallen out of bed. With Jake gone, and him once again between therapists, Maura had had to go to Hank for help lifting him back into bed. Not exactly the image he'd wanted to give one of his employees. Especially one as tough and long-lasting as Hank.

"Bridle break?" he asked uneasily.

Hank looked back at the corral, took his sweat-stained hat off and scratched his balding head. "Ain't enough time to keep up with it all. Roy's almost ready to head out to work on the fence lining Morton's place. Gonna take him a good three days to get it all repaired."

Seth shifted in his chair, hesitant to voice his question because of how shamefully he'd behaved. "Bring them here and I'll see what I can do."

If Hank was surprised, he hid it well. "Sure enough, boss. Be right back." The old cowboy turned on his booted heel and walked away, then returned five minutes later with an armful of bridles, harnesses and a toolbox from the tack room holding all the necessary equipment for the repairs.

Seth accepted the lot through the window, conscious of the old man's gaze on his. "Thanks, Hank."

Hank grunted. "Mighty good to see you gettin' back to your old self. Let me know if you need anything else."

With a nod Seth watched Hank amble away.

Hank had worked the ranch since Seth was born, and he hadn't realized how much of a load had fallen on Hank's battered shoulders until now. The cowboy hadn't let him down, though. Before his accident, times had been hard and he'd had to let several younger men go and take up the extra load himself. Roy helped out there as well.

But now he wasn't out there working alongside Hank and Roy, the men he'd fired hadn't been rehired, and Jake couldn't lend a hand considering he had to drive to Helena a couple of days a week to keep his own job.

Guilt smacked Seth upside the head. Jake insisted on spending money on him. Equipment, whirlpools, therapists. But none of the expense would be a waste if he'd cooperate and make it worthwhile. *If he tried harder.*

Seth swiped a hand over his face and glared down at the bridles, then sorted through the tools. First things first. He'd take care of the tack—then worry about the other things that needed fixing. Himself included.

Maybe since everyone was so determined he would walk again, it was about time he regained some of that faith in himself.

CHAPTER SEVEN

GRACE HURRIED OUTSIDE. "Lexi? Lexi, are you out here?"

The little girl hadn't been waiting for her in the living room like usual. Maura was in her bedroom working on a cross-stitched baby blanket with her feet propped up to combat some swelling in her ankles. Jake was at work. Seth once again ensconced in his room. So where was Lexi?

She'd searched the house, listening closely in case the child had begun playing an impromptu game of hide-and-seek and forgotten to tell her. Checked the bathrooms, the closets, the pantry. She wasn't there.

Shielding her eyes, Grace scanned the yard, her gaze settling on the barn. Even though Lexi had brought the kitten into the house to live, that didn't mean the child wasn't out playing with the rest of them in the tack room. *Of course.*

Grace hurried toward the structure and pulled on the heavy barn doors—could Lexi have opened them? The darkened interior gave her pause, but she shook off her unease and stumbled inside the dimly lit barn, running halfway down the aisle until she heard Lexi giggling.

She slowed her pace, then stopped, breathing heavily. Lexi's laughter floated out of the tack room again, and Grace pressed a hand to her racing heart. Lexi was fine. Everything was fine.

"They sure like you."

Roy Bernard's voice drifted through the air, low and soft. Grace bolted down the length of the large barn to the end where the tack room was located. Inside she found Lexi on the floor surrounded by a halfdozen kittens. Bernard sat on a stool, watching her.

"Lexi," she rasped. "I've been looking everywhere for you."

Bernard stood, his smile widening when he saw her. "We've been here waitin' on you. Nice to see you again, Grace."

She couldn't say the same, not when the man's gaze tried to strip her bare.

"Lexi, your mom made Jell-O. Your favorite. There's a bowl just for you in the fridge already set up with whipped cream."

"Oh, yay! Come on, Grace!" The kittens forgotten, Lexi ran out of the tack room and down the expanse of the barn, her feet thumping against the hard-packed earth.

Grace glanced back to Bernard. Lust radiated from his eyes, and he licked his thick lips as though in anticipation. "I'm glad you came to see me."

"I came to find Lexi."

Bernard stretched out a hand and braced it against the door frame, leaning toward her. "But now she's gone and you're still here. Must mean something."

It meant she should've had the sense God gave her to not be caught alone with him. Grace took a step back, keeping her gaze on him all the while.

"Where you goin'?" Roy asked, falling into step in front of her, close enough he could reach out and grab her. "You know, Earl always talked about how sweet you were. How he had to watch you real close to keep the boys away. He said you were a tease."

Fear ate away at her, black and cold and bone-weary deep as the past battled with the present. *He didn't know. He couldn't.*

She backed through the door so she wouldn't be trapped inside, casually sliding her hand along the jamb, the wall of the barn, to guide herself. The rough-hewn wood prickled her palm and she flinched when a splinter found its way beneath her skin.

Bernard stalked her. "So what about it? You free this evening? We'll drive into town, eat. Maybe go find us a nice quiet spot?"

"Grace, come on!" Lexi called from the barn's entry.

She wasn't alone. He couldn't do anything with Lexi right there. "Coming!" Grace kept moving. "I've—I've got to go." She turned and jogged to where Lexi stood waiting impatiently. As soon as Lexi saw her coming, she darted away.

"Grace."

Bernard's voice came from behind her, within a few feet, and she whirled around, a strangled shriek emerging from her mouth because he was so close when she'd practically run the entire length. How had he moved so quickly? So quietly?

"We going for a drive?"

Come on, Grace. Let's go for a drive and see what we can see.

Shoving her stepfather's voice aside, she squared her shoulders. "I—I don't date anyone involved in my patients' lives. It…isn't good practice. Since I never know how long I'll stay."

Bernard didn't buy it and the look on his face said so, but Grace didn't care. Seeking only escape, she hurried out of the barn and caught up with Lexi in the foyer of the house as the little girl struggled to remove her boots.

Unable to help herself, Grace grabbed hold of Lexi's shoulders and swung her around. "Did he…what were you and Roy doing in the barn?"

Lexi's eyes widened. "I was playing wiff the kittens."

Grace pulled Lexi a step closer and dropped to her knees to meet the child at eye level. "Honey, listen to me. Did he—did Roy touch you? *Did he?*"

Lexi's blue eyes filled with tears. "Am I in trouble?"

Oh, God. Grace bit her tongue to keep from giving in to the fear and rage inside her. The memories. What was she doing? "No, honey, you—you're not in trouble. I'm being silly. That's all."

She forced what she hoped was a comforting smile to her lips, but her throat burned hot. Nothing had happened and here she was frightening a child.

"Lexi, don't—don't go outside or to the barn without telling someone. Never again, okay? You scared me because I couldn't find you."

"'Kay."

Grace shook her head. "I mean it, Lexi. Someone needs to know where you are at all times. I told your mother I'd watch out for you and here I didn't know where you were. You do *not* step outside without telling someone. *Promise me.*"

"I promise," she repeated dutifully, her little hand lifting and rubbing against Grace's cheek. "What's wrong? Why're you crying?"

Grace smoothed a hand over Lexi's curls, loving the way the silky-soft spirals wrapped around her fingers. She had to get hold of herself.

Nothing had happened.

"Nothing's wrong. I was scared when I couldn't find you, but so long as you always tell someone where you're going I won't worry again, okay?"

Lexi nodded, her cheeks rosy from the cold air outside. "Can I play in my room?"

"That sounds perfect," Grace murmured, pulling Lexi onto her lap and hugging her quickly before helping the child take off her one remaining boot. "I'll come up in a bit to play with you and we'll work on the pumpkin later."

"Okay, I'll go make us a tea party!" Lexi ran across the foyer and scrambled up the stairs. "Don't forget the Jell-O!"

Grace watched Jake and Maura's daughter until she rounded the curve of the stairs and disappeared out of sight. Alone, she reached out a shaky hand and grabbed Lexi's coat off the floor. Pretty and pink. It reminded her of her bedroom in Earl's house.

The vise around her chest returned.

In and out. Slow, deep breaths. She would not have a panic attack. In and out. Sniffling, she closed her eyes and shook her head firmly. *Nothing* happened.

Nothing happened, Grace. You always remember that, you hear? Nothing *happened.*

A sob caught her by surprise and Grace clamped

a hand over her mouth to squelch it. In and out. Slow, deep breaths. In through the nose, out the mouth. Concentrate. All she had to do was concentrate. Lexi was fine.

Fine, fine, fine.

You're fine, Gracie-girl. Mighty fine. Too fine a tease for anyone but me.

AFTER SHE PULLED HERSELF together, Grace took the Jell-O and a handful of cookies to Lexi's room and urged the child to feed her myriad of stuffed guests. While Lexi arranged her miniature tea set, goodies and friends, Grace walked down the hall to Jake and Maura's bedroom.

The door was open and she saw Maura inside still working on the baby blanket, a concentrated frown on her face as she contemplated her stitches. Grace knocked, then entered as Maura looked up with a smile that quickly faded. "Grace? Are you all right? What's wrong?"

"Lexi's in her room preparing for a tea party." Grace shut the door, leaving a small crack so they could hear if Lexi called. "But…Maura…I don't know how to ask this or even if I should because I know it's none of my business, but—"

"Whatever it is, say it. You won't offend me."

She inhaled deep, sick to her stomach still. "Have you ever talked to Lexi about…improper touching?"

Maura drew in a sharp breath. "What *happened?*"

Grace explained how she couldn't find Lexi and how Lexi had been alone with Roy Bernard in the barn. She stressed that the child had been playing with the kittens, but she made no effort to disguise her fear that Lexi needed to be watched, that *all* children needed to be watched, and informed, of danger.

"Anyway, the thought struck me and I wondered and I thought, if you haven't spoken with her, maybe over the tea party you could talk to her using the dolls and—"

Maura placed a comforting hand over her bulging stomach and caressed, her expression sad and more than a bit shocked. "It never occurred to me to— I mean in the city where children are abducted, sure, but here—"

"It can happen anywhere."

Maura looked up, her gaze sharp.

Grace averted her eyes and studiously looked about the room as though fascinated by the decor. "Nothing happened and I certainly don't mean to scare you," she assured her. "But I had the thought when I saw Lexi there by herself with him and—"

"Of course. She's young, but she needs to be aware of strangers and her surroundings. The tea party is perfect, Grace. Thanks for suggesting it.

And I'll talk to Jake so he can discuss this with her as well. She needs to hear it from both of us."

"Where is everybody? I'm ready!"

"We're coming, Lexi, hang on!" Maura set the blanket aside and sat up. "Grace, you've listened to me rant and I appreciate it so much, but I want you to know if you ever need to talk—"

Grace laughed, the sound high-pitched and awkward as she grabbed the doorknob and pulled. "Thanks, Maura. L-Like I said, I wondered if you'd ever said anything to Lexi. That's all."

"Grace—"

"That's all, Maura. I'm, uh, going for a walk now."

SETH LOOKED UP FROM his task as Grace let herself into his room. He tossed the bridle and bit aside and wiped his hands on the towel in his lap. "You're late."

"I didn't know we had an appointment."

He indicated the checkerboard he'd set up earlier. "Thought you'd be here sooner and we might play a game." He put the lid on the tin he'd been using and tossed it into the toolbox on the floor beside his wheelchair.

Grace slowly walked over to the chair still in position across the table from him. "I went for a walk."

"You came back over an hour ago. Maura had to

bring me my lunch while you were gone." He wheeled himself closer to the table and waved a hand to indicate she had the first move.

"As much as you grumble about not being hungry, I'm surprised you noticed." Seating herself, she nudged one of the red pieces with her finger.

He'd noticed, all right. Maura had brought his tray in and scampered right back out the door. She'd barely spoken to him, unlike Grace, who carried on a constant stream of chatter to fill the silence. He'd been surprised to find he missed it. Her.

Then again, maybe not so surprised.

He'd seen her walking along the road back toward the house and she'd looked so lost and alone and sad, her expression touching a place deep within him he'd thought long hardened against her. But her expression—

He knew darkness and pain. Despair. He knew what it was like to hurt in a way indescribable to others, and apparently so did Grace. Instead of her usual sure stride, her gait was stiff and awkward. Hesitant in a way he'd not have associated with his confident physical therapist, but characteristic of the past and belonging to the girl she'd been.

"Your turn."

He stared at her bent head, then pulled himself away from his thoughts long enough to counter her third move. He slid another checker forward. "Ever hear of rattlers? Might be cold, but there could still be a few strays out warming themselves in the sun. We've even seen a mountain lion or two. Coyotes on the hunt."

She didn't comment.

"Heard you with the weights in the gym. You exercise enough for ten people. Makes me wonder what you're trying to outrun."

She flinched at his comment. Not an obvious movement, but enough to make him realize he'd hit a nerve without trying.

He took in her flushed cheeks and red-rimmed eyes and frowned. "Brent okay?"

"He's fine. And exercise is good for you. A great form of stress relief."

Seth glanced down at the board and his frown deepened. When they'd dated, Grace had been a mean checker player, but now it was pretty obvious her mind wasn't on the game. He jumped and took two of her pieces. "What're you stressed about?"

Now that he'd taken control of the game, Grace sat up and appeared to pay a bit more attention as she considered her options. "Nothing."

"Must be something."

She shrugged. "I already spoke to Maura and—"

"About what?"

Sighing, she lifted her fingers to her temple and

rubbed. "I just— I wondered how safe it was for Lexi to play unsupervised on the ranch. That's all."

Seth stilled, focusing on her averted gaze. "Something happen?"

"No. But like you said, there's the risk of animals. She's so small they'd think she was prey. Plus the risk of her playing with something she shouldn't play with. Not knowing exactly where she is…I mean…she is still a little girl and—"

"What happened?"

With a single finger she pushed one of her checkers. "I couldn't find her today when I left you. She wasn't where she was supposed to be and—it scared me. That's all."

"Where was she?" He'd heard Lexi's footsteps traipsing up and down the stairs so he knew she was home, safe and sound. At least now. But what about before Grace had found her?

"In the barn. She was with the kittens and…Roy Bernard."

He stared at her, wondering what the problem was. "If she was with Roy, then she wasn't unsupervised. Lex was probably bugging him to take her riding."

Her head jerked up, every trace of color draining from her face. "She rides alone?"

"No, she's never ridden alone—she just turned five years old. But you said she was with Roy and

I'm sure Roy kept an eye out for her. Everyone on the ranch does. Now, what are you beatin' around the bush about? Had she been in the stall with the stallion? She's been told to stay out or she'll get stomped."

"She wasn't in the stall," she rasped, still pale. She fixed her gaze on the board between them, wide-eyed but completely unseeing.

"In the loft? She's part monkey, she climbs up there all the time. She's been told to stay out of the rafters, but sometimes she still goes up there when she's upset. I wouldn't be concerned—"

The color she'd lost was now back. Two circles of blazing crimson scorched her cheeks, but instead of giving her pale skin some relief, the redness compounded the problem because it was so unnatural.

"Look, Grace, if she's all right, why're you making her being in the barn out to be such a big deal?"

She slapped her palms down onto the table. "Because I don't think it's a good idea for a little girl to be alone with a strange man!"

The checker pieces scattered from their squares, a few bounced into the air, but even though he was aware of it happening, Seth couldn't take his eyes off her face. Or remove himself from the images her words conjured up.

Grace closed her eyes, took a deep, shuddering breath—all of which made his body turn hot, then cold, terrified at the thoughts flying through his mind.

"You want—" He had to stop and clear his throat. "You want to elaborate on why you feel this way?"

Her gaze was on everything in the room but him, and he wasn't going to jump to conclusions even though his mind was coming up with all sorts of ugly scenarios on its own. He took comfort in the fact that if something had happened to Lexi, Grace wouldn't be in his room playing checkers. He held on to that knowledge with both hands and tried to stem the panic racing through him on Grace's behalf.

She swallowed, the sound audible in the quiet room, and if she squirmed in her seat anymore she was going to fall out of it. Finally, eyes closed, she shook her head. "Seth, I'm sorry. I shouldn't have hit the game or—or blurted that out. I'm overly tired and—I got scared when I couldn't find her, and then when I did, it made me question her free run of a ranch as big as this one. That's all."

That wasn't all. Fury blindsided him. Sickened him. Obliterated all other thoughts. Lexi might be fine, but Grace certainly wasn't. The fear in her expression, the quiver in her voice. She tried to hide them but couldn't. Heaven help him—

He rubbed a hand over his rough face, images tumbling through his head faster than he could keep up with them. Grimacing, he was unsure of what to do. He needed to keep Grace from bolting, and if he pressed her, she'd do just that. No, he had to keep her with him and talking. Get her to trust him.

He fingered the bristly beard covering his jaw and an idea surfaced. One that would bring her close to him, not allow her to hide. He had to find out more, even though he wasn't sure he wanted to learn the truth.

"Lexi told me a while ago that I looked like the picture of Father Time in one of her books."

Her eyes locked onto his beard and the corners of her mouth turned up in a sad attempt at a smile. "Did she?" she asked, her tone painstakingly polite. "I guess your looking different was something else for her to get used to."

He rubbed his jaw again. "It was easier after the accident to let a beard grow, but now it's itchy and a nuisance."

Grace glanced down, her fingers shaking as she retrieved the red and black chips that had scattered when she'd smacked the table.

"You keep harping on me moving around more, but I think I'd be more inclined if I felt like my old self again. You know, get rid of this beard and cut my hair." He let that bombshell drop and paused before adding, "Don't want to go into town, though, and Maura would butcher me if I asked her. Can't do it myself."

He sensed her surprise and he couldn't blame her. He wasn't a man who asked for help, his pride wouldn't let him. But in this case, with Grace, his pride didn't matter. He needed the truth, and the only way he was going to get it was to get Grace to open up to him. Let down all those barriers she'd kept between them ten years ago whenever he'd tried to get close. The same barriers he saw protecting her now. But to do that, he needed to let down some barriers, too. And for the first time since his accident, he was finally ready to do just that.

She shrugged, the movement stiff. "Maura c-cuts Jake's hair?"

"Yeah, but she's too nervous around me. And her back's always hurting. Jake said he has to rub it about every night to give her some relief. I can't ask her."

Grace nibbled her lip and fidgeted again. "Are you asking me?"

"Yeah. I'm asking you."

CHAPTER EIGHT

AN HOUR AND A HALF LATER Grace awkwardly stood with one foot between the metal foot supports of Seth's wheelchair, and scraped a disposable razor blade over his lathered jaw. It had taken a while to cut his hair, but the pile on the plastic garbage bag she'd placed on the floor of his bedroom attested to a deed well done.

Seth wanted his hair short and close to his head for easy maintenance, so she'd cut the length with scissors before putting Maura's clippers to use, leaving the top a bit longer than the sides and nearly biting her tongue in two trying to get it even.

That done to the best of her ability, she'd started on his beard and cropped it as close as possible to make it easier to lather and shave, something she'd thought he'd do himself. But somehow she'd wound up with the razor in hand and getting more and more nervous now that she stood face-to-face with him instead of behind him cutting his hair.

Seth's nearness, the way he watched her from beneath his absurdly thick lashes, made it difficult to concentrate on the task, and even harder not to remember them as they used to be. How he'd pull her to him and kiss her, hold her close as they walked.

Thankfully, the scrape of the razor filled the awkward silence between them, but the spicy lather she'd smoothed onto his jaw filled her senses with its tantalizing masculine scent as she removed the outer layers of Seth's despair. She gradually unearthed the changed man beneath and found herself staring at him, her shaking fingers moving slower, slower.

Seth had always been a man's man. Large, tall, his body muscular. But now his angular face was more finely honed, his weight loss painfully evident but not unattractive.

Preoccupied, Seth lifted his chin to give her better access to his neck, and the move placed his mouth near hers. Warmth unfurled in her lower extremities, surprisingly strong and overwhelmingly hot, and she shook her head and sighed. She'd been there nearly two weeks and the stress of battling Seth must have taken a toll if she'd already forgotten how things had ended between them. She'd never be able to be the woman Seth wanted.

"What are you thinking?"

Her gaze slid to his, so close, and the very air around them stilled. After a long, breathless moment, she returned to shaving him and silently berated her hand for trembling worse than before. "Nothing."

"It must be something important the way you're frowning."

She finished scraping one side of his jaw clean of whiskers, rinsed the razor, then tipped his head to the other side. Once in position, she dropped her free hand to his shoulder to secure her balance, and the heat of his body burned her fingers through the material of his shirt. She snatched her hand away and curled her fingers into a fist, resting it on the handles of his wheelchair instead.

"Come on, spill. What are you thinking about?" Seth pressed as he shot her a glance that made her pulse pound. She fought off a wave of panic and told herself she was being foolish. Hadn't she learned from her mistakes?

Seth was a handsome man, no doubt about it. Now that his hair had been cut and his beard was nearly gone, he looked more like the man she'd wanted more than anything to spend her life with, but couldn't.

"I'm curious," he continued with an enticing murmur. "We've talked about me every day since you got here, but I know very little about what you did once you left."

"I thought subjects that personal were off-limits,"

she countered, referring to his refusal to discuss his life with Arie. "Anyway, there's not much to tell— stop moving," she ordered when he raised a brow at her words and the muscles of his face pulled.

"I think there's plenty to tell. But if you don't want to talk about that, there's always the time before you left when you and Brent lived here with your dad. We could talk about that."

Not commenting, she scraped the razor over his jaw two more times.

"What about college, then? Any exciting stories?"

Definitely a safer subject. "Not really. I was too busy working, studying and trying to keep Brent and me fed. We lived in an apartment the size of a shoe box and I worked during the day, went to school at night."

"What about Brent?"

"He went with me usually, hung out in the back of the room and did his homework. When he was old enough, he worked, too. Whatever he could do to make ends meet and help pay his engineering tuition."

"How'd he decide on engineering?"

She fought her impatience. "He tagged along with me, remember? Guess he got tired of me and my patients complaining about the lack of devices on the market for the mobility-impaired. He liked figuring out ways to solve the problems I run across."

Grace's heart picked up its pace, pounding out an impossible rhythm that made her light-headed. She used her fingertips to tilt his head away from her, but just because Seth wasn't looking at her didn't mean she wasn't aware of him.

The lather didn't disguise the soft stubble that remained on his face. A shiver ran all the way to her toes as her mind ever so kindly supplied a mental image of his chin rasping against her skin. The feel of his lips, his tongue. She choked back a moan of unease.

It took three attempts by her shaky fingers, but she finally cleared the curve of his chin without a nick.

"Am I making you nervous?"

"No," she answered sharply, too sharply, thanks to the sensations whirling through her body. *Those* made her nervous.

She wasn't a woman ruled by bodily desires. She'd spent too much time—years—suppressing those kinds of thoughts and curiosities while making herself stronger. Better able to defend herself against the male species in general, who would always be bigger and stronger and—

"Why're you biting your lip, then?"

She released the flesh from between her teeth and

flicked her gaze to his. She had to put a stop to this insanity now. Ten years ago she'd tried to pretend nothing had happened. Tried to be a teenage girl with Seth for a boyfriend. It hadn't worked then and it would certainly never work now.

"We are not discussing me."

What happened to the man who'd simply refused to go to therapy? The man who'd made her angry and upset because he wouldn't fight for his recovery? Him she could handle, but this—this inquisitive, overtly sensual cowboy was too much. Too much like the Seth she'd known and loved.

"Why not?"

"Ethics."

"Meaning?"

She sighed deeply. "It's self-explanatory, isn't it? You're a patient, I'm your therapist. We had a past but broke up, and it doesn't matter now, anyway, because *ethically* we shouldn't discuss personal things, not unless it concerns your recovery, which means," she continued when he opened his mouth to protest, "my personal life will not be discussed, just as yours with Arie won't be. Now stop asking."

Seth cupped her elbows in his hands, taking her by surprise as he drew the razor well away from his face. Her breathing hitched in her throat, the heat of his hands marking her as his rough, callused thumbs scraped gently against her skin.

"What if I've changed my mind? What if I want something more personal again?"

Back and forth. His thumbs smoothed over her flesh as his tone wound around her in a way that brought both comfort and tension at the same time. The tension she understood, but comfort? Comfort was the last thing Seth could give her. Not when her past stood between them.

"What if I want more from you, Grace?"

She'd always regretted the way she'd left and wanted to make things right between them. But even though she'd once thought the second job she'd taken waitressing nights and holidays to pay for counseling sessions would've made a difference in how she regarded herself when it came to moments like this, it hadn't.

Funny how reality had a way of smacking her in the face when she least expected it. Seth wouldn't want her at all if he knew the truth. No matter how compassionate, he was still a man. And no man wanted something—some*one*—dirty.

"We aren't discussing me."

His expression became even more inquisitive. More determined. "Your favorite color still pink?"

"Seth—" A humorless laugh escaped before she could stop it. She *loathed* pink. Which he well knew having come to her house one afternoon to surprise her, only to find her burning her pink comforter, pillows. Everything pink she'd been able to bring out of the room where her stepfather—

"We aren't discussing *me*."

"My favorite color is green…like your eyes," he murmured. "You have the most amazing eyes, Grace. Dark green like the pines, gold flecks shining like the sun through the needles. Beautiful."

She tried to pull her arms loose from his hands and those darned thumbs, but couldn't find the strength. Finally, after looking down and seeing the disturbing sight of his skin against hers, she raised her gaze to his and immediately regretted it.

Because *his* eyes, his warm, molten, whiskey-colored eyes, revealed far too much of his feelings and thoughts. His intent. The lines around his mouth creased, and she wanted to touch them, smooth her fingers over them and pretend for a moment she was someone else. A different person, a different woman.

"Not pink, then. What color do you like best of all?"

She faltered and it took her a moment more to concentrate. "Red," she muttered dazedly.

Seth tilted his head to the side, the sexy smile still in place. "Now was that so hard? You'd look good in red with your dark hair and eyes. So why do you always wear black or gray?"

Black blended, gray was nondescript. Both colors disguised and minimized and hid. "No reason."

His fingers flexed the slightest bit, his thumbs blessedly still. "Everything's a secret with you. Makes me wonder why, darlin'," he murmured. "So what do you say?"

She stared at him. "To what?"

"To…talking to me again."

"We're talking," she whispered.

"No, we're chatting like strangers, but we aren't strangers, are we?" Gently, he drew her closer. "Are we, Grace?"

"I'm your th-therapist."

He chuckled, the sound husky and rough. Seductive. "But if I recover, then you won't be. I'll just be a man again."

Seth would never just be a man.

"One who never understood the real reason why you walked away from me."

She tried to pull away from him, but standing the way she did, his hands still holding her, she couldn't. "This curiosity you're feeling is nothing more th-than gratitude. For making you get out of this room and fight back when everyone else let you bully them into leaving you alone."

He lifted a hand and stroked a long finger down over her cheek, near her mouth. "That's a crock, honey. Yes, for the first time in a long time I want to get up in the morning. I want to watch you play with Lex and see you smile because it's about the only time you really smile, but how I feel has nothing to do with gratitude."

She licked her lips to wet them and nearly moaned aloud when his eyes caught the movement and flared, burned. "Y-You're thankful Jake finally got a therapist you couldn't s-scare away."

"But I do scare you, don't I? Why, Grace? Why were you so afraid back then? Why are you so afraid now?"

"Let *go*."

"I'd never deliberately hurt you. I've been angry and a bullheaded jackass, pissed at you and the world, but I'd never, *ever* hurt you, Grace. You know that, right?"

She laughed, but the sound was low, torn from within her and full of emotions she couldn't hide. She closed her eyes and fought for patience, prayed for strength. Lifting her lashes, she stared into his dark, dark eyes and battled against the empathy she saw. The gleam of knowledge.

No. He couldn't possibly—

"You care for me, Grace, otherwise you wouldn't be here. I know it and so do you. Don't you?"

Grace tried to form the words to deny his claim. She'd learned not to get too involved in her patients' lives, because if she did, it always hurt more when it was time to leave. But what about Seth? Jake and his family?

Lexi had wormed her way into her heart so fast she hadn't had time to build a defense, and like Jake, Maura was proving to be a sweet and wonderful friend, whereas Seth—

What *did* she feel for him? Two weeks of fighting him, eating with him, passing time with him, sleeping next door to him night after night. It added up. She'd spent more time with Seth than some couples spent together in months. "I d-do care about you, but not—not in the way you mean," she insisted.

Uh-huh. That's because she'd never stopped loving him. With every meal they shared, every talk they had and every story he'd told her about his life, his ranch and his irrepressible niece, the feelings she'd already had for Seth had deepened even more.

Fear washed through her and she called herself every kind of a fool. "Seth—" Her shoulders drooped. "I'm here to help you fight this chair. To be a *friend* during one of the worst times of your life." She held up the hand holding the razor when he opened his mouth to interrupt her. "Please, hear me out."

He nodded reluctantly.

"I don't give in to your tantrums. I don't pity you. I don't cater to you, and since your accident that probably makes me different than the other people you've had around you. The fact that we had a past complicates things, but the psychiatrists say it's perfectly natural for a patient to think it's more. To think that it's...s-sexual or spiritual or whatever, but it's *not*."

She forced her gaze to meet his. Forced herself to hide the truth. "What you think you feel for me is nothing more than gratitude."

With his hands on her arms he gently tugged her closer, then, in a surprisingly lightning-fast move, brought her the rest of the way so he could press his mouth to hers. "Not quite," he murmured against her lips.

His mouth was firm and warm. His tongue hot and wicked, seductive, as it sought access. She resisted, but then he gently nibbled her lower lip, and she gasped in surprise. He pressed the advantage, the kiss sweet and deliciously enticing at the same time.

Momentarily helpless, she leaned into him as Seth rubbed and caressed and kissed her with a skill she could associate only with him. He teased her with his tongue, soft, questing forays into her mouth to remind her of days gone by. He made a sound deep in his chest, a mix between a groan and a growl, and used his hand to angle her head more to his liking.

Oh, the man could kiss. A distant part of her mind registered the *clink* of the plastic razor falling to the floor. She didn't care, though. Once the razor was gone, her hand fell to his shoulder and heat seared her. Seth's fingers slid into her hair, massaging, nudging her head this way and that with tiny movements that allowed the sensations spiraling between them to soar.

He ran his callused hand down her neck, over her shoulder, down her arm to the fullness of her breast.

And she remembered.

Tension made her stiffen. Fear overcame her, smothered her, as her mind confused the pleasure she received at Seth's touch with pain and a darkened bedroom. Pretend trips to town where her stepfather pulled off into the woods and—

She heard a whimper and vaguely recognized it as coming from her throat. Her fingers dug into the flesh of his shoulders, desperate to hold on to the sweet, pure passion of Seth's kiss a bit longer, but it didn't work. With the feel of his hand against her breast, the images intruded again.

She tore her mouth from his and jerked away when her stomach pitched wildly. She scrambled backward, away from Seth, away from the past, hot, dizzy. She gagged. Icy cold sweat drenched her body and made her quake.

Earl had told her, warned her. *Taunted* her. Said he was the only man she'd ever have because she'd never be able to let another—

Grimacing when her stomach rebelled again, she had to fight down bile by swallowing repeatedly. Earl was there, always there, looking at her, touching her. *Raping* her.

But for a moment she'd experienced desire from Seth's touch.

Not shameful, not abusive, just...desire.

"Don't run away from me, Grace. Come on, sweetheart, talk to me—"

She shook her head back and forth, her hair swinging with the motion and falling over her shoulders in a loose wave. When had he removed the band?

"Seth, you can't ever, *ever* do that again."

She could feel his eyes on her as she fought to breathe, wrapping her arms around her stomach, trying to make it stop hurting, trying to make herself invisible.

She licked her lips and released a soft moan of frustration when she tasted Seth. Remembered heat mingled with the fear and she winced at her body's confusing responses. How could she be so frightened and so—so *aware* of Seth at the same time?

"Grace?" Seth rolled himself closer to her, searching her face for answers. "Honey, come here. Sit down. Talk to me. What's wrong? Why are you shaking?"

She lifted a hand and rubbed her fingers against

her temple and forehead, struggling for calm. For distance. "Seth, I mean it—"

"You kissed me back," he argued, daring her to deny his words. "It was sweet and hot and sexy. You liked it until…until I touched you," he said deliberately.

"Don't."

"You liked it, I could tell."

She closed her eyes in unmitigated shame.

You're a whore. You like it when I do this. You like it!

Step after step she retreated until her back hit the door. "As your therapist—"

"I want more than a therapist." Seth moved closer. "I want you. I've always wanted you. Please, *talk* to me."

She ran a hand through the hair falling over her cheek and shoulder and pushed it back out of her face, wincing when her fingers caught in a tangle.

"Here." Seth held her hair band out to her and she stared at it blankly. Their fingers brushed when she snatched it and shoved it onto her wrist, ignoring the perceptive expression on his face stating he knew exactly what she thought, what she'd felt.

"Honey, you don't have to be afraid of me."

A tremor ran through her. She wanted to run, get out of his room and hide somewhere until she calmed down, but the adult in her, the one who'd had session after session to learn to cope with this moment, demanded she stand and fight.

You have to face the past to move beyond it.

"I don't want you pawing me."

"Pawing you?" His features changed, became even more tender, and tender on Seth was a hard thing to ignore.

"I didn't *paw* you. I touched you and for a moment you liked it—until something happened." His gaze sharpened. "What were you thinking about then?"

She shook her head mutely.

"Did it have anything to do with your dream last night?"

Her *dream?* She choked out a laugh as she shook her head again, denying his words, denying her thoughts.

"I hear you, honey. Night after night, I've listened to you. You whimper and cry out. Wake up screaming and terrified. So much so you can't even stay in your room. You roam the house trying to escape whatever's bothering you."

The air rushed out of her lungs. "This—this isn't proper behavior between a patient and therapist."

His voice was filled with determination. "I wouldn't call arm wrestling your patients for therapy privileges exemplary conduct, either. Or locking them out of their rooms."

"Seth—"

"I already owe you one session. Come on, talk to me and I'll give in. You can work me until I drop—all in the name of therapy."

"My dreams are none of your business."

"You want me to cooperate?"

Now he was blackmailing her? His tone dared her to neglect her responsibilities. Dared her to talk to him. To be honest. "Why are you doing this? I don't need a patient pretending to be a shrink."

"Ever talk to anyone about your nightmares? How long have you had them?"

She leaned her head against the paneled door behind her. "Give it up, Seth. Please."

"Who hurt you?"

Her eyes locked on his as Seth rolled closer and lifted his hand to touch her. She flinched backward, her head banging against the door. He murmured something soothing, then brought the fist he'd captured to his lips and placed a gentle kiss on her knuckles.

"Let me go." Her mind knew better than to tell. She'd held it in for too long, guarded her secret too well. "Let it go, *please*. You can't turn back time or change the past," she challenged desperately. "It won't change anything between us."

"No…but maybe it would help you."

She yanked her hand out of his grasp and turned,

tugging on the doorknob. Seth's wheelchair blocked the way, but she managed to open the door enough to slide a leg through.

She hated her past. Her memories. Herself.

"I'm not asking these questions to hurt you, honey. But I am asking you to take a risk like I'm taking a risk."

She stared at him, half in and half out of the door. "What are you risking?"

"I risk getting my hopes up that I'll walk again when there are no guarantees. I risk you walking out of my life *again*."

No words came. Not even denials.

"Have you ever considered what it would be like to tell someone what it is you're keeping bottled up inside? Ever think about how nice it would be to let your secrets go and not have to worry about them anymore because they wouldn't have a hold on you?"

Dear God Almighty, yes.

"Earl Korbit couldn't have been an easy man to live with. He kept his distance around town, but when he did come in, he got drunk with his buddies and left trouble behind."

She laughed, husky low. *Trouble* didn't begin to describe Earl.

"He played with a rough crowd. They probably hung around the house, too. Did one of them hurt

The Harlequin Reader Service® — Here's how it works:

NO POSTAGE
NECESSARY
IF MAILED
IN THE
UNITED STATES

BUSINESS REPLY MAIL
FIRST-CLASS MAIL   PERMIT NO. 717-003   BUFFALO, NY

POSTAGE WILL BE PAID BY ADDRESSEE

HARLEQUIN READER SERVICE
3010 WALDEN AVE
PO BOX 1867
BUFFALO NY 14240-9952

Get FREE BOOKS and a FREE GIFT when you play the...

LAS VEGAS
GAME

Just scratch off the gold box with a coin. Then check below to see the gifts you get!

YES! I have scratched off the gold box. Please send me my **2 FREE BOOKS** and **gift for which I qualify**. I understand that I am under no obligation to purchase any books as explained on the back of this card.

336 HDL D7ZA   **135 HDL D72C**

FIRST NAME	LAST NAME

ADDRESS

APT.#	CITY

STATE/PROV.	ZIP/POSTAL CODE

(H-SR-10/05)

7	7	7	Worth TWO FREE BOOKS plus a BONUS Mystery Gift!
🍒	🍒	🍒	Worth TWO FREE BOOKS!
🔔	🔔	♣	TRY AGAIN!

www.eHarlequin.com

you?" His voice lowered, barely a whisper, raw with emotion. "One of them hurt you, didn't they? One of them raped you."

Tired of the questions and the battle, exhausted by the tension, Grace found herself nodding.

CHAPTER NINE

THROUGH THE ROARING in her ears, Grace vaguely heard Seth's vicious curse. It didn't matter, though. She squeezed the rest of the way through the door and raced down the hall to the front of the house, all the while ignoring his bellows to come back.

On the porch steps, she pulled the hair band off her wrist and captured her hair into a ponytail, desperate to get away.

"Grace, what's wrong? Where are you going?" Maura called from somewhere behind her. "Are you all right?"

She waved a hand, unable to turn around because of the tears blinding her. "I'm going for a run," she choked out.

"But you'll freeze in this wind! And it'll be dark soon!"

Freeze? She was burning up inside. She shook her head and kept going. Down the long driveway, past the barn and outbuildings, farther and farther away from the house. All the while wishing she could pack up and leave.

Maybe she was like the others. When push came to shove, Seth had proved to be a master at getting rid of his therapists.

What right did he have to question her?

Her thoughts raced too fast for her to concentrate on any particular one so she focused on emptying her mind instead. Her breath formed white puffs in the air around her as she pushed herself faster. Harder. Her legs pumped out an impossible rhythm she didn't have a prayer of maintaining.

After a mile she told herself she needed to turn around and go back. She kept running.

At two miles the images in her head began to take shape and she gasped for breath, remembering the threats. The slaps.

The pain of Earl pushing himself inside her.

She dug deep and kept going. Every stride longer than the last. She was stronger now, able to fight back. And she'd survived.

She'd done what she'd had to to live through the horror and keep her promise to Brent. She'd kept her mouth shut so she and Brent could stay together and not abandon each other the way their mother had abandoned them.

Then Earl had died and she'd been freed, *spared,* but by then it was too late. The damage had been done, and she'd been pretending all these years. Pretending to live and breathe. Pretending nothing was wrong and she'd recovered. Pretending to be strong. She was twenty-seven years old and never had a real relationship except for Seth, and she'd handled that so badly.

Since then there'd been a handful of dates who'd called her cold because she'd never let them get to her. Never let them get close. And the one time she'd tried—

She shuddered, remembering her companion's horror when he'd been getting into things and she'd shoved him away in time to hurl on the apartment floor.

Grace groaned and continued to run, unable to go any faster but determined to distance herself all the same. Then she simply stopped, gasping in pain as her body pitched forward onto the road and she threw her arms out to catch herself. Fire pierced her hands as the gravel cut into her skin, but it was nothing compared to the hurt in her heart. A burning blaze she couldn't escape no matter how hard she tried.

She rubbed her palms together to ease the pain before wrapping her arms around her stomach. She'd go for a month, sometimes two, in peace. Then she'd come home from school and find Earl drinking, waiting. He'd stare at her, watch her every move with a look on his face—

You don't tell. Somebody finds out and you'll be sent away because you ain't mine. Brent'll stay, though. He'll stay here with me, and what'll happen to him without you, Grace? Think things will be easy for him?

"No," she whimpered.

You're not my daughter. Your slut mother assured me of that. But you look like her and act like her. You even talk like her. She liked it like this, and so do you.

"No."

This is our secret. I'll kill that pathetic whelp of mine you love so much if you tell. I'll kill him and make it look like an accident. All you have to do is keep quiet.

"No!"

Grace reeled where she sat. Curled so tight she couldn't breathe through the vise around her chest, mentally fighting the battle she'd lost too many times to count. Her stomach churned and rolled. She pitched sideways in the road and vomited.

SETH STARED AT THE BOWED head of his niece and frowned. Lexi had taken a good look at him when she'd walked in the room behind Maura, but after she'd smiled in response to seeing his shorn hair and missing beard, she'd begun to pout and refused to lift her chin from her chest. He felt like a monster. Mainly because that's all he'd been to her since coming home from the hospital.

He ran a hand over his face, still surprised to find it smooth, and thought of the woman responsible. He hadn't meant to drive Grace away. Quite the opposite. He wanted her to trust him, confide in him.

Weeks ago he feared never walking again, but now his fear had changed. Grown into something else. What if Grace left?

"Any sign of her?"

Maura shook her head. "I called Jake so he could look for her on the way home. Hank, too, in case she ran in that direction. Roy was in the bunkhouse. He said he'd take a walk and see if he could find her."

"Thanks. Let me know if you hear anything."

"You yelled at Grace."

Seth's heart ached at Lexi's accusing tone. In response, Maura gently pushed Lexi forward, and Seth looked up in surprise when he realized she was leaving.

"Maura…"

"You're on your own, Seth. You're good at arguing with women and sending them running, so you explain it."

He stared at her, somewhat shocked to find his normally timid sister-in-law angry enough to bring up the past. What had Jake told her about his and Arie's last words?

Obviously not the truth.

Maura retreated into the hall and closed the door

behind her, leaving Seth to fend for himself. He smiled. "Yeah, sweetheart, I did. But I'm sorry about that and want her to come back, but until she does, I wanted to talk to you. To try to explain why I've—" he paused and cleared his throat "—why I've been so mean to you."

"You don't like me no more," she said simply.

Seth inhaled deeply and sighed as he waved her closer. Lexi took a couple of steps, but no more.

"That's not true. I love you, Lex. I love you so much I...I didn't want you to see me because it made me sad to see you sad."

She ducked her head low again, her fingers twisting together into a knot.

"You understand?"

Lexi began swinging back and forth while standing in place, the full skirt of her purple corduroy dress twirling around her calves. "You still like me?"

Seth smiled and closed the distance between them, careful to move slowly so as not to scare her. He grasped Lexi's tiny hands in his, noting the dimples on her chubby little fingers had mostly turned into knuckles sometime in the past year.

What other things had he missed because he was too busy feeling sorry for himself? Fighting anyone who tried to help him and pushing away the people who loved him most? He owed it to Lexi to get better and be the example Grace reminded him he was. He also owed it to himself.

"I loves you, Lex," he murmured, deliberately adding the "s" because the first time she'd told him she loved him, she'd done the same. They'd said "loves" instead of "love" ever since.

"I loves you, too, Uncle Seff."

Six little words. How could six little words mean so much? Things were going to be different. Starting now. She loved him, despite his yelling at her, despite his treatment of her, she still loved him. Amazing.

"I know you do, honey, and I'm so sorry I hurt your feelings. I'm going to be better from now on."

Lexi looked up at him, eyes wide. "You got your breath back?"

Seth paused at the strange question. "What do you mean?"

Lexi bit her lower lip. "Grace said when you was ready to try to get better it was like getting your breath back after you fall down. That you had to wait till you felt better 'n' then you'd try. Did you get it back?"

Leave it to Grace to understand. "Yeah, baby, I guess I did. But now we need to talk about something else. I hear you've been running around and not telling people where you're going."

Head back down, Lexi nodded. "I scared Grace bad. She cried."

And now he knew why. Seth nodded, struggling to find the right words, his jaw so tight it was a wonder his teeth didn't shatter. It was a sick world when kids had to be warned about things like personal safety. Something Grace knew first-hand.

"From now on I want you to *always* let an adult know where you are and what you're doing so one of us can come with you and keep an eye on you."

"But you don't go out 'n' play anymore." She smiled shyly, peeking up at him from beneath her lashes. "If you come I'll wait for you to catch up."

This time the lump in his throat threatened to choke him. He'd wasted such precious time. "Step on my feet and climb up here."

Lexi grinned from ear to ear and placed her booted feet on his. Seth frowned when he thought he sensed pressure, then shook his head at his imagination. He knew it had been a rough day when he imagined feeling again.

But maybe the sensations were real? Either way he wasn't sure. He certainly wasn't going to mention anything and get his hopes up.

Lexi scrambled onto his lap, giggling as she threw her arms around him. He returned the embrace, then swung his wheelchair around in a circle and laughed as Lexi squealed, long and loud. Heaven above, he'd missed that sound.

"Do it again! Do it again!"

He pressed a kiss to Lexi's forehead. If only Grace were here to see him getting his "breath" back. He owed her, needed to thank her for getting him to realize what was most important.

He turned his wheelchair around until it faced the window. Outside, the driveway stretched into the distance, empty. Where was she?

Better yet, when she returned, what would he say to her?

GRACE CAME UPON THE CABIN by accident. Chilled to her core, she staggered toward it, remembering Maura telling her about the key hidden under the flowerpot. She'd stay for a bit. Warm up and stretch out the cramps in her legs.

She shivered again and another cramp in her calf made her groan. She was close enough to the house she could have gone there to shower and warm up, but she wasn't ready to return yet. Not when her thoughts were so torn and jumbled, her emotions raw and exposed.

Finding the key, Grace opened the door and her breath caught as she pushed the weathered wooden door wide. There were paintings everywhere. Hung three and four high on the walls, over the mantel, set atop the sparse furnishings. They even lined the narrow stairs that led to the loft Maura had mentioned. And all of them were gorgeous.

Some bright and colorful. Some black-and-white sketches. Gallery-quality. And all the product of Seth's extremely talented wife. The one he wouldn't discuss.

Without really wanting to, Grace stepped inside and shut out the wind, hugging herself for warmth until she saw a throw tossed over the back of a love seat. She picked it up and wound it around her shoulders, sneezing twice from the dust.

Several crocks held a multitude of brushes ready to be used. Paint-spattered towels were neatly folded and set aside. A container kept charcoal pencils orderly. The drawing beside the box of pencils drew her attention and she stared at the cowboy for a long moment, studying Seth's lean form as he worked with a colt. The drawing's angles and planes captured Seth's masculine grace and magnetic pull. Drawn by a loving hand.

Determined, Grace tore herself away from the sketch and studied the others. Animals, landscapes, portraits. Rather than having a particular leaning, Arie was talented at capturing every image she attempted.

Grace's lips twisted. She drew stick people.

So why are you comparing? You shouldn't be and you know it because there is no comparison.

Frowning, she turned and made her way to the stairs, following the myriad of images up to the loft where a twin-size bed was shoved up against the far wall. Paintings covered every available space there, as well, the most precious piece being one of Lexi.

The portrait had been painted when the little girl was only a few months old, dressed in angel wings and a smile, a white blanket covering her hips. It dominated the others, hanging above the bed without anything crowded around it.

The wind whistled and a *bang* sounded, startling her until she realized it was the porch swing hitting the outside wall of the cabin. Grace looked out the tiny loft window and noted dark clouds lining the distance.

She had to go back. She didn't want to cause anyone upset or worry, but how would she ever face Seth again?

Grace pulled the throw tighter around her shoulders as she made her way back down the stairs. With one last glance around the cabin, she left, careful to make sure the door latched and the key was back where it was supposed to be.

Another shiver coursed through her and she had the strangest feeling she was being watched, a fact proved true when she stepped off the porch the same time Roy Bernard walked out of the shadows beneath the pines. Grace stopped, her entire body tensing in unease.

"You all right?"

"Fine. I was just heading to the house."

"I'll walk with you."

"No, that's not nec—"

"You too much of a snob to walk with me?"

"It's not that at all, it's just…I'm not very good company at the moment." She stepped forward with a purposeful stride, hoping to escape the cold and Roy as quickly as possible.

"Earl used to talk about you."

Her ankle twisted on a rock as she misstepped.

"He used to tell me things…things buddies tell each other."

She swallowed back the lump of fear in her throat. Earl wouldn't have told anyone what he did to her. He wouldn't have risked getting caught or charged.

"Pretty girl like you shouldn't be crying. Seth tell you off like he did all the others?"

"Patient information is confidential. I can't talk about his case."

"Then how 'bout we go back to the bunkhouse and talk about something else?" Roy asked, his gaze roaming over her body with a leer she saw all too clearly in the shadows of the evening light. "I'll make you feel better in no time, and then you can go back to the house and give Seth a what-for, knowing what it's like to have a real man."

She smelled the alcohol then. Roy wasn't drunk,

but he was well on his way, and with the scent and Roy's words came another wave of torment and fear.

She broke through the trees and into the clearing not far from the house. The bunkhouse was close by, mere feet away, and she hurriedly put some distance between her and Roy as the man stumbled along the path behind her. Rough laughter reached her ears when he noted her hasty rush.

"You change your mind, you let me know, Grace, you hear? We'll have us a good time you an' me. A mighty fine time."

IT WAS HALF PAST MIDNIGHT when Grace opened her bedroom door as quietly as possible and slipped into the hall, making her way to the main room in her sock-encased feet. Being unable to sleep came as no surprise, but, taking a cue from Seth and locking herself in her room after her confrontation with Roy, she'd wound up pacing the floor until everyone turned in, avoiding Maura and Jake's knocks at her door, and trying to cope with Seth's revealing silence.

Seth didn't come to check on her, and the fact he made no attempt after what she'd revealed to him spoke volumes. Just as she feared, he hadn't been able to handle the truth.

Like that was a surprise?

"'Bout time you joined me. Now, don't take off,"

Seth ordered when she stopped and glanced long-ingly over her shoulder at the darkened hallway be-hind her.

"It's not easy being on this side of the door, is it? Patience isn't one of my best qualities, and it's about killed me to sit here and wait for you to come out of your room."

She stared at him, the light from the fire soften-ing his angular features but doing nothing to dis-guise the worry and upset etched in every muscle.

"How'd you get out of bed?"

"Never went. You're not the only one having trouble sleeping tonight."

And it was her fault. "Go to bed, Seth."

"We don't have to talk. We can just sit here and keep each other company."

She was tempted. She didn't want to return to her room, didn't want to be alone. Didn't want to stare at the walls since her mind had a tendency to superim-pose Roy's face over Earl's after the dash from the cabin.

Hesitantly, Grace stepped forward and tried to re-press her fear.

"I'm sorry, Grace."

What happened to not talking? And what was he sorry about? Sorry he'd upset her? Sorry for being so stubborn? Her shoulders stiffened and anger flared again. If Seth's being sorry had anything to do with pity, he could take his "sorry" and shove it up his—

"For everything. I'm sorry for everything, all right? The way I've acted, the way I brought up your past. Maybe I should've realized sooner, but I didn't. I'm not used to talking about these things, so if I sounded insensitive, it's out of ignorance and nothing else. I'm sorry."

He turned away from the fire, the look on his face revealing a torment that mirrored her own. In his eyes she saw regrets, sorrow for things said and done, pain and disillusionment.

She ambled closer and dropped down onto the couch closest to the fire, propping her elbow on the arm and leaning her head against her hand, her legs curled up underneath her.

Seth swung himself away from the hearth and slowly rolled over to where she sat. She watched him from beneath her lashes, uneasy, waiting to see what he'd try next after the disastrous kiss that afternoon. But when he did nothing more, she turned her attention to the glowing flames and tried to relax.

After the grandfather clock in the entry chimed once and she didn't think she could stand the waiting any longer, he finally broke the silence.

"Did you think I'd abuse you? Is that why you

ran away when I...when I pressed you for more and hinted I was going to propose?"

She'd always known he'd never abuse her. But she'd still had to leave North Star. She'd had to do all the things her mother hadn't—she'd educated herself, steered clear of men who wanted to control her, made herself independent and strong.

"Earl was killed in a construction accident, wasn't he?"

Seeing the inevitable about to unfold, she braced herself for the questions as best she could and nodded. "He was drinking on the job and fell off a roof. His head hit a block."

Seth grimaced at the image, and Grace shifted on the couch, all the while aware of Seth's presence beside her. Warm and comforting and strong.

"I don't want your pity, Seth. I survived—and I'm fine," she insisted even though she knew it was a lie. If she was fine she wouldn't be up in the middle of the night having this conversation.

"Whatever you say to me stays with me, Grace. Including what you told me earlier. You can talk about it with me."

He couldn't even say it. *It.* Now she was avoiding the word. *Rape.* Molestation. Assault. Whatever the title, it was all the same. All brutal. All unforgettable. Unforgivable. She closed her eyes and sent up a prayer for strength.

"I don't want to talk about the past."

Seth touched her shoulder, lightly smoothed his fingers over the material of her robe and rubbed. "It's nice and dark here, isn't it? So different from the daytime when Lexi's running around screaming and everyone's busy dealing with problems and worries."

"No, Seth."

"I'll make you another deal," he murmured. "Just like the deals you keep coming up with to get me to go into the gym."

"I said I don't want to talk about this."

"But I already know, so you don't have to hide any longer, right?" His voice was gravelly and rough, coaxing. "Why not talk to me?"

"Because you're my patient."

"I was your boyfriend first," he countered. "So it's okay. During the day we'll be therapist and patient like you want. You can order me around and get me back on my feet, boss me to your heart's content. But at night when neither of us can sleep, we'll talk," he continued, "in the dark. As friends. No one will ever be the wiser."

Like that would work. She sighed and settled her body deeper into the leather cushions. She didn't raise her head from her hand, didn't look at him.

"You've never told anyone, have you?"

She had trouble swallowing because her throat was so dry. Grace closed her eyes and tried to separate herself from the words, but it wasn't possible. The wound, even after all these years, was still too raw. Because she hadn't dealt with it?

"And Jake obviously doesn't have a clue, otherwise he probably wouldn't have asked you back here, knowing the memories were bound to crop up."

She dipped her head low and rubbed her temple as she shielded her profile from him. In and out, slow and easy. It was getting harder and harder to breathe. The room was too hot.

"Was it a friend of Earl's? One of his construction buddies?"

The crackle and pop of the fire was the only sound in the room. That and the slight, humorless sound she made at Seth's question.

CHAPTER TEN

GRACE SENSED MORE THAN saw the action. Felt the movement, *felt* Seth's stare as reality set in. Now the disgust and horror would come. The excuses.

She didn't look at him. Didn't move. She'd learned early on how to hold herself perfectly still, unmoving, so that Earl would grow bored with her lack of response, and whatever he did, whether with his fists or his body, would be over quickly and with as little pain as possible.

"It was *Earl?*"

A small nod was all she could manage. Her heart pounded out of control, blood pumping past her ears made Seth's voice seem to come from far away. She strove for calm, prayed for help, and slowly, oh so slowly, her heart began to ease its frantic pace, her breathing became less ragged. At least her counseling sessions had given her something.

The weekly visits had gone on for years, but no matter how hard she tried, she'd never been able to confess all. Her counselor knew by the way she avoided the gritty details, but the reality was she'd never said the words aloud. If she did, it made it real, not just a nightmare she couldn't escape.

"It wasn't incest," she murmured, licking her dry lips. One hand hid her from Seth, her other arm wrapped tightly about her legs and pulled her knees to her chest. "Earl wasn't my biological father."

"As if that makes a difference." Seth lifted a hand to tenderly stroke her hair. She shouldn't have allowed the contact, told herself to get off the couch and away from him. But in the darkness his touch was exactly what she needed to get through the night and the story he seemed so determined to hear. She stared into the flames, confused by the urge to tell Seth everything. To blurt it all out and get rid of the poison inside her.

"Brent is Earl's child, but I'm not." She laughed softly. "Thank God I'm not."

His fingertips barely moved, gentle against her scalp. "How did you find out?"

A shuddering sigh escaped. "The accident. You were on the rodeo circuit then. I remember reading about one of your wins while Brent was in the hospital."

"How'd it happen?"

Orange and red colors danced with blue in the hearth, hypnotic, mesmerizing. "We were leaving him, but my mother crashed and in the accident

Brent got pretty banged up, a broken arm, pins in one of his legs. He'd always been a small, sick kid, but then Earl went over the edge. Said she'd 'ruined' Brent for good."

Seth's stroking touch continued, giving her strength.

"We stayed at the hospital a lot. Stayed away from Earl. But then Brent was released and we had nowhere to go. That's when she admitted to Earl I wasn't his. Brent and I heard her. Then I saw Brent's expression and realized what he already had. She'd only told Earl the truth because she was so desperate, she *wanted* him to kick her out, and me, even if it meant leaving Brent behind."

Seth seemed to understand her need for contact without making a big deal out of it. His fingers rubbed little circles. In her hair, soothing. On her neck and shoulder, a vain attempt at easing the tension.

"Sometimes I can still hear her screams, the sound of his fists as they hit her," she said, numb. "Flesh hitting flesh makes a funny sound, you know? Different from when you hit bone. Anyway, he beat her up, threw her out and she…never came back to get us."

The vise around her chest returned and Grace struggled for control. She heard the counselor's voice in her head, a nice woman she'd chosen because she couldn't handle the thought of telling some strange man. A man who'd look at her and possibly let his mind wander to the things Earl had done.

Grace panted and tried to hold back her emotions, vaguely hearing Seth's murmurs to take it easy. Relax. Take slow, deep breaths. His arm surrounded her shoulders, but she didn't feel trapped by him. No, in that moment, in the dark and in his arms, she was protected.

"Easy, honey. Oh, God, help her. Grace, calm down, you're okay," he soothed, kissing her hair, her forehead. "You're okay. Breathe, honey, breathe."

She swallowed, wet her lips to moisten them even though her accelerated breathing dried them right out again, and prayed for the dizziness to go away. She heard Seth talking, whispering nonsense that meant nothing and everything at the same time. Soothing and tender.

"Good. That's it, Grace, nice and slow."

A small sound escaped her, a half laugh, half cry. Seth muttered something under his breath, but she couldn't make out his words. Instead she took the moment for what it was and closed her eyes, relishing the feel of his arms around her.

With her dates, she'd been more inclined to simply get *through* the good night kiss or hug rather than enjoy them. Seth was different. His touch had always been different.

After a long while, after the fire had burned down and lost some of its warmth, Seth shifted. "I told myself all afternoon I wouldn't ask for details, that I wouldn't push you to answer questions—but I want to understand."

Resigned, she nodded, the move giving him silent permission to ask whatever he wanted. The burden was beginning to lift, slowly but surely. It wasn't gone, not by a long shot, but there was a part of her that was free for the first time ever.

"When did it start, Grace? How?"

His hand stroked her back. Up and down, slow, easy caresses. "You can tell me anything. Remember that. Anything at all, let me help you." Seth shifted so that he was closer to her, his hand massaging her neck. His other hand covered her fist, and she felt his tension. His rage.

A shudder racked her. "It was that same night. After she'd told Earl the truth. He came into my room. I was thirteen, almost fourteen."

A blistering curse filled the air. Seth pressed her close, held her and placed a long kiss to her forehead. Two. Three. Four kisses. His breathing was ragged, his body hot. Grace turned her hand over, loosening her fist, and he immediately laced their fingers and squeezed. As if hearing the words hurt him as much as Earl had hurt her.

He pressed another kiss to her forehead. Her hair.

A half dozen kisses that, in that moment, helped her more than the counseling sessions. Helped her realize she was still a person. Still worthy of gentleness, kindness and—

"Keep going. Tell me all of it."

She couldn't look at him. She shut her eyes and buried her nose against his shoulder. If Seth pushed her away in disgust afterward, at least she'd always have this moment of safety and security. This moment of comfort and caring. She hadn't known how badly she needed it, either. To be held while she said the words aloud.

"I usually slept downstairs, Brent upstairs. But when we brought Brent home, we switched rooms. The next day Earl didn't acknowledge what he'd done. He'd kept his h-hand over my mouth and warned me to keep quiet. Said it was my fault because—because I l-looked like my mother."

"You are *not* at fault," Seth growled. He caressed her face with his broad hand and lifted it so that she had to look him in the eyes. "Tell me you didn't believe that son of a—"

"I didn't," she whispered hoarsely. "I *don't*," she stressed, lowering her gaze. "But he said horrible things. That he'd loved her and she'd ruined everything good in his life. That it was only fair that he got to r-ruin me."

"You aren't ruined, Grace. You hear me? Yes, he hurt you, he raped you, but he didn't *ruin* you."

"I couldn't stop him."

His Adam's apple bobbed as he swallowed. "I know, honey, I know. But it's not your fault. You were a little girl."

"I didn't tell," she continued, the desire to confess all too strong to ignore. "I didn't leave. Brent was hurt," she choked. "He was only nine."

"He depended on you," Seth soothed.

"After the fight, after what our mother said, Brent knew I wanted to run away but he begged me not to leave him. And I knew I couldn't tell anyone because they might split us up into different homes. Or maybe take me and leave him." She laughed bitterly. "And if someone came to the house to check out the situation and *didn't* take us away…" She shook her head. "I couldn't risk it, Seth, don't you see?"

"Yes," he murmured. "I understand, Grace. You did what you thought was best to protect Brent."

She shifted slightly but Seth made sure she didn't pull too far away.

"Did Earl abuse Brent?"

"Not sexually. Earl definitely liked women." She shrugged. "I was young but tall and big for my age, as tall as my mom."

"Don't make excuses for him," Seth argued.

"Don't belittle yourself." He stroked her hair, pressing a kiss against her crown. "Did Brent know?"

"No. When the casts came off we switched rooms again. My room was right next to Earl's."

Seth winced. "How long did this happen? How long did he abuse you?"

That was the question she'd dreaded most. To say it out loud made it seem even more shameful. More pathetic. She'd always thought it wouldn't happen again, that the next time Earl came to her room she'd be able to stop him. Only she hadn't.

"Th-three years," she finally managed to say, her voice so low she wondered if he heard her. He couldn't ask her to say it again. She couldn't.

Seth pressed another kiss to her forehead, the muscles of his arms and chest trembling all around her. "It didn't stop until Earl's death?"

She laughed, the sound strained. "I never imagined being so happy because someone died. I even made a cake." Another laugh burst from her lips, the sound high-pitched. "I told Brent it was in case someone came by but we c-cut it and ate it ourselves."

"It's understandable, Grace. Anyone would've behaved the same. But you can't let the past keep hold of you forever. You've got to stop punishing yourself."

"I know that."

"Do you?" he murmured. "Because you're going to drop soon unless you come to terms with what happened."

She shut her eyes as though that would block out his words, let Seth hold her for a moment more before she forced herself to pull away from him. "I'm fine now. I *am*."

"You exercise until you're so tired you think you can crawl into bed and not dream, don't you?" He reached out and put a hand on the nape of her neck, tugging her toward him.

The gesture was loose and easy and not in the least bit overpowering, so Grace let herself be guided back against his chest. Let herself bask in his warmth and solidity.

"I know what that's like," he continued. "When Arie died, all I could think of was what I should've done, how I should've felt. Lying in the hospital, I had a lot of time to think—and all I could think about were the mistakes I'd made. Wonder if my accident was my punishment for not being the husband I should've been. Guilt's a hard thing to overcome, Grace, and it's something I understand. We can forgive others, but when it comes to moving on and forgiving ourselves we aren't nearly as generous."

Oh, was that ever true. "The nightmares stopped for a while," she said. "But when Jake kept calling, wanting me to come back to North Star to be your therapist, they started up again."

He squeezed her tight. "You came, anyway."

"Some demons have to be faced."

She'd always blamed herself for not being stronger. For not fighting harder. For being so afraid. But Earl's construction-worker fists had been vicious and sometimes it *had* been easier to let him have his way, because she knew she wasn't going to win the battle. Because the punches and slaps hurt too much. For her and Brent both.

"Grace, when you're with a man, do you panic? Is that why you pulled away from me when I kissed you?"

She used her hands against the arm of the couch to shove herself from him once again. This time he let her go.

"Okay, okay," he said, holding up a hand. "It's too soon for another revelation, I get it. You're off the hook for now."

Her gaze narrowed. "What do you mean for now?"

His smile was both tight and teasing. "I mean for now, it's obvious you don't want to talk anymore so I'll give you some space." He caught one of her hands before she could snatch it away and his thumb brushed over the top, back and forth, slow, tantalizing sweeps of work-roughened skin. "Come on, I'm hungry. Let's go get a snack."

She'd bared her soul and he wanted to eat? "Seth, you can't just—"

He dropped her hand and placed a finger against her lips. "Trust me. You've shared your secret with me and now I'm going to reward you by letting you in on a top-secret Rowland family recipe for the ultimate midnight snack."

Unable to stop herself, she smiled weakly. "Top secret?"

Seth winked at her. "Uh-huh. Chocolate chip oatmeal cookies, vanilla ice cream and hot fudge topped with whipped cream."

He was trying to distract her. That's why he'd eased off on the questions, to give her breathing room. But what did Seth feel? Did he want her now? Or was this whole teasing, snack thing his way of distancing himself from her? A way to give himself space? She needed some space herself. Time to celebrate this milestone. She couldn't think anymore, which meant there was only one thing left to do.

"Race you to the kitchen."

CHAPTER ELEVEN

THE FOLLOWING MORNING Seth wheeled himself through the house, unable to shrug off the tension between his shoulder blades. He entered the foyer as the phone rang, and since it was barely light outside and Jake and Maura hadn't ventured downstairs yet, he swung himself around and headed to the kitchen.

It took two tries to reach the phone, but he grabbed it off the base on the third ring, nearly tossing himself out of his wheelchair in the process. His foot slipped off the rest but got caught between the two metal flaps, and a dull stab of pain shot up his leg.

He faltered, stunned. Pain?

Seth stared down at his foot until the voice on the other end of the phone line registered. "Anybody there? Hello?"

"Rowland Ranch," he murmured distractedly into the receiver.

Silence filled the air for a moment. "Hi, uh, yeah, is Grace Korbit there? This is Brent, her brother. Is this Jake?"

Seth settled back into his chair, stuck the handset between his shoulder and head to hold it and readjusted his foot onto the rest.

No pain, no feeling. Nothing. But had it been something? He remembered the feel of Lexi's boot on top of his foot and hope shot through him. Maybe it was progress, but maybe it was his imagination playing one heck of a trick.

Please, God?

"Hello? If this is a bad time—"

"No, this is Seth. It's fine, sorry, I was distracted."

"Oh, okay. So how's it going? Sorry to hear about your accident. Grace isn't working you too hard, is she?"

"Not too bad. She's still asleep, though." And he wasn't going to wake her up, not after the emotional night she'd had.

"Oh, man, I forgot the time difference. I didn't wake *you,* did I?"

"No, I've been up awhile."

"Good. Hey, sorry for the mistake. I was hoping I could tell her some good news, but it'll wait." Brent's excitement was tangible. The guy sounded as if he was bouncing off the walls.

"I could use some of that myself right now."

"Ah, you *will* appreciate this! Grace might not have mentioned it, but I'm an engineering student at Duke and I've been working on some designs to help Grace's patients. Anyway, I sold one of my inventions," he said, followed by a whoop of laughter. "The company wants to look at a couple of others, too. I got enough of an advance to fly Grace home for Christmas. If it's okay with you," he added abruptly.

Seth smiled at Brent's enthusiasm. "Congratulations. But I have a better idea. Why don't you surprise Grace and come here? You can stay with us. There's plenty of room."

"Cool, man, thanks. I'd love to see Montana again. I appreciate the invitation. It's been three years since Grace and I've spent Christmas together. She's always somewhere working and money's been a problem with me in school and having to buy my equipment, you know?"

"Money problems are something I can identify with," Seth said.

"Listen, a buddy just walked in to study. We've got finals coming up, one's two days before Thanksgiving, can you believe it?"

"Good luck. Call back when you get your flight information and I'll make sure someone's at the airport to pick you up."

"Thanks again. It'll be really cool to surprise her. I'll probably fly in the week before Christmas. If that's okay?"

Seth chuckled. "That's fine. Maybe when you get here you can tell me more about your inventions."

"Sure thing. Hey—anything in particular you'd like to be able to do but can't?" Brent questioned suddenly. "My best ideas come from her patients."

Next to walking again there was only one thing he wanted to do. "Got an idea of how to get me back on a horse?"

"Huh," Brent murmured, surprise lacing his voice, "that's a new one. I'll give it a shot and see what I come up with." Brent tossed out a goodbye and hung up.

Seth replaced the receiver and waited, wondering if he'd feel something again. He closed his eyes and smacked his leg, but when nothing happened, he fought his disappointment and turned himself around. Time, the docs said. He'd heal in time. So if their words were about to prove true, he had to be ready. And what better way than to toss himself into physical therapy with Grace, dig Jake out of the paperwork and do something productive?

"Seth?"

Maura stood behind him dressed in a bathrobe and slippers, her hair fuzzy, her expression priceless.

"You know, Maura, I've been thinking," he said, smiling when her eyebrows arched in response to his tone. "You and Jake were ready to move out before my accident. You must've been disappointed when that didn't happen."

She crossed her arms over her chest, confusion etched on her features. "A—A little."

"What about now?"

"What about it?"

"Would you like to move into the studio? It's small, but—"

"The studio? You mean it?"

Seth wheeled himself close to her. "I know it's been hard, and all I can say is that I'm sorry. I've behaved like an idiot. You've given up a lot for me and I appreciate it. I thought maybe you might want a place of your own, you and Jake and the kids."

Maura's hand trembled when she lifted it to cover her mouth. "I can't believe—Jake said you'd never offer the studio because it was Arie's."

Seth frowned at her choice of words but didn't question her. "Yeah, well, I'm offering. You want it?"

"Yes! Oh, yes, I do!" She leapt toward him as fast as a pregnant woman could move and wrapped her arms around his neck. "Seth, thank you. You've helped us out so much already and I know it's selfish of me to want more, but thank you, thank you, thank you!"

Seth returned her hug, grinning. "No problem. I should've said something sooner."

Maura squeezed him before pulling away. "Seth, about Arie…and what I said when I brought Lexi to see you—I'm sorry. I should never have said what I did, implying that you upset her so badly and let her drive. I have no business butting in on your marriage, and her accident wasn't your fault."

He acknowledged her words with a nod. "It was true, Maura. We did have an argument before she left, and I didn't stop her. I didn't even try."

"But *she* was the one at the wheel, not you. I know how Arie could be. Here I was practically accusing—"

"It's fine, Maura. It's all in the past," he murmured, uncomfortable. Her expression softened at his words, then quickly changed to one of worry. "What, you don't believe me? What's wrong?"

"Nothing. But you've made this wonderful offer and I don't think Jake will agree to move. He always says there's no need."

Seth patted her arm, then gripped his wheels and turned his chair toward the foyer. "So change his mind," he said with a wink before leaving the kitchen and Maura behind.

GRACE WAS IN THE GYM finishing up some notes in Seth's file when he wheeled himself into the room. After last night's conversation she'd wondered how she'd face the awkwardness of the day, and this was it.

"'Mornin', honey."

Her head jerked up and she met his gaze, stiffening in her seat. "Don't call me that."

"'Mornin'?"

She closed the file with a snap.

He chuckled softly. "You're prickly this morning. Mad because I kept you waiting on breakfast?"

Prickly? Grace frowned. Her anger surprised her, and the rational side of her brain wondered why. Seth had been kind and gentle and tender last night. Everything she could've asked for as she'd revealed her soul. So why was she angry?

"Something wrong?"

She rubbed a hand across her forehead. "Headache," she muttered, knowing before she said it that the excuse was a lame one.

"That's understandable. You had a late night."

"So did you."

"Yeah, but I've spent most of the past few months sleeping. I can lose a few hours. You, on the other hand, needed to sleep in."

He rolled closer, and she studied him from beneath her lashes, angry with herself for being so weird. He acted fine, normal. Actually, he behaved better than normal considering he'd ventured out of his room without coercion not only last night, but this morning as well. She'd gone to his room to wake him, but he wasn't inside.

"Where have you been?" Seth looked ready to

burst with energy, edgy to get started on his therapy like they'd discussed.

One side of Seth's mouth lifted in a sexy grin. "Around. And it's okay, Grace. Relax."

"What's okay?" Maura asked from the doorway, a heavily laden tray in her hands.

Grace jumped up and practically ran across the room to take the tray from the pregnant woman, ignoring Maura's protest. "You shouldn't be carrying these trays. I told you I'd come get it after you kicked me out of the kitchen."

Maura's laughter filled the air. "It's not that heavy. And besides, I had to come see Seth again since I'm still having trouble taking it in. Thought I was seeing things when I saw him working in the den. Have you been in there? He made it through nearly all the paperwork. Everything's in neat little stacks like it was before Jake got hold of it and scattered it to kingdom come. I didn't go in because I was too afraid of scaring him off." Maura shook her head, grinning all the while.

"Watch it or I might change my mind about the studio," Seth warned, the twinkle in his eyes belying his tone of voice.

"Studio?" Grace repeated numbly, feeling much like an observer at a tennis match as she glanced back and forth between the two of them.

"I, uh, figured Jake and Maura must be getting

tired of not having their own place," Seth explained, rubbing his palms over the rounded arms of his wheelchair. "So I told Maura this morning she and Jake could move in there if they wanted."

Maura nodded vigorously, tears in her eyes. "I still can't believe it. Seth, thank you again. I know how much Arie loved the studio you built her—"

"It's yours," Seth interrupted. "So did you convince Jake?"

Maura blushed, her freckles standing out with prominent detail. "Not yet. But I'm working on it," she said with a playful smile.

"Jake doesn't stand a chance, you'll be moved in in no time."

"I hope so. And Grace," she murmured. "I don't know how to thank *you.*"

"I didn't do anything."

"Oh, yes, you did," she countered, a definite bounce in her step as she left the gym.

Suspicion filled her as she faced Seth. "How did you know Maura wanted the studio for her and Jake?" She carried the tray the rest of the way to the table.

"I guessed?"

"Try again."

This time she noted he didn't bother to pretend. "I overheard you talking one day when I had my windows open." He raised a brow. "You were trying to come up with a scheme for getting me to agree but weren't sure what to do. Don't know why you didn't simply ask."

A rush of heat filled her cheeks. "Maybe because you'd been behaving worse than a hibernating bear? I can't believe you listened in on a private conversation."

He chuckled. "A man has to do whatever it takes to stay ahead of the females in his house. Especially when we're outnumbered."

"Here's the other tray." Maura scurried into the room, left the tray on the table and hurried back out again with only a pleased grin and a thumbs-up.

Seth's rich laughter filled the air. "Eat up, Grace. You'll need the energy for our therapy session."

A WEEK LATER SETH CAME upon Grace rocking back and forth in one of the chairs on the front porch, her hands shoved deep into her pockets.

"I've been looking for you," he said from behind her.

She started and turned, and he watched as she took in his appearance. Unlike the pajama pants he'd worn since his accident, today he'd dressed in jeans, a flannel shirt, coat and athletic shoes.

"What do you think?"

A smile hovered at the corners of her mouth. "It's okay."

He laughed and continued to watch Grace as she tried to rock her way to Texas, amused that for a woman who knew him so well, she was extremely nervous around him.

Grace looked pretty sitting there, her hair loose and flowing over her shoulders, a sleepy look on her face. Dressed in worn jeans, a thick cream sweater, black coat and boots, she looked a lot different from the woman he saw in the gym every morning and afternoon.

"Pretty day," he murmured, finally breaking the silence. "You, uh, wanna go for a walk?" He waited until she glanced over at him, then performed a quick wheelie, one of the new moves he'd conquered during the past week. "I've got wheels and can travel."

She smiled at his joke and even released a soft, husky laugh, and he knew he'd made progress. Definite progress.

"Sure you're old enough to drive that thing?"

He winked at her and watched as she blushed. "Just watch me. Come on, walk with me." Strangely nervous, he waited for her answer, which came in the form of a nod and her standing up.

Seth hid his pleasure as he took the ramp off the porch and Grace walked down the steps. By silent agreement they passed up the barn and the memories it contained, and simply toured the grounds around the house.

In back, Grace braved the spiders down in the cellar to retrieve a couple of apples for them to eat while they made their way to the creek. They strolled through the clearing to the water's edge. Grace sat on a rock and watched the rippling current while he sat in his chair and watched her, unable to take his eyes off the sweet beauty of her face and the fragile woman he glimpsed beneath the tough exterior.

Emotions rolled inside him. Some good. Some really bad.

GRACE SLOWED FROM A JOG to a walk as she headed back down the road toward the house. The air smelled like snow and had a bite it had previously lacked, so she knew it wouldn't be long before the ground was coated in white.

The sound of a motor came around the bend behind her, and she glanced over her shoulder when the vehicle slowed and pulled to a stop. Jake climbed out of the passenger side of a ranch truck, and with a shiver of unease, she noted Roy Bernard's smirking presence at the wheel.

"Hey!" Jake slammed the truck door, and Roy slowly pulled away, smiling as he tossed her a salacious wave. Grace ignored him.

"Thought I'd walk back with you," Jake said, falling into step beside her. "And congratulate you.

I can't get over the change in Seth. You've worked a miracle."

"It's no miracle, Jake. Seth's finally ready to move on, that's all. I didn't do much of anything."

"Uh-huh." His tone implied he didn't believe her. "Regardless, I haven't seen him like this since, well, I don't know when. A long time. Before Arie lost the baby. It's amazing."

Jake's words stabbed a place deep in her heart, and like it or not, she was curious. Much more than she should be. "I saw pictures of her—Arie—in Lexi's room. She was beautiful."

Jake nodded. "Those pictures are the only ones in the house. Seth boxed them all up after the crash, but Maura insisted those stay." Jake kicked at a rock in the road.

She wanted to ask him a million questions, but something held her back. Did she really want to *know* how much Seth loved his wife? Want to think about him living and sleeping with someone else? Someone talented and beautiful and—

Jake glanced over at her, his expression serious and very much resembling Seth's. "Anyway, thanks to you, Seth's coming out of it, working in the office, fixing the tack. And now his therapy's going great. I couldn't believe it when I heard you telling him not to overdo instead of having to fight to get him to do anything."

Leaves crackled and crunched beneath their feet and they walked for a little way in silence before Jake looped his arm around her shoulders and matched his pace to hers. "I owe you more than I'll ever be able to repay, Grace. Me and Maura both. She really likes you. She needed someone here, you know, to confide in and talk to. I'm afraid she's right, sometimes I don't get it."

Grace chuckled. "You never did," she said with a smile. "And I like her, too. You did good. I just feel sorry for her."

"Hey!"

"I'm not kidding," she teased. "I'm glad you found someone willing to put up with you."

He squeezed her shoulders. "Ha-ha-ha. But as you're so amused, let's talk about you."

"No thanks."

"What? After seeing how well you and Seth are getting along again—"

"*Jake.*"

"I can't help but think it sure would be nice to have you as a sister-in-law."

Her gaze narrowed. "Has Seth been talking to you about me?" Oh, now there was a mistake. Why did she have to ask *that?* "Forget I said anything."

"Not a chance." Jake's expression turned to one of pure delight. "So Maura and I aren't the only ones wanting this, huh? There *is* more to Seth making a comeback." He practically did a little jig there in the road.

"Stop that!"

"He's a good guy, Grace."

Like she didn't already know that. "I never said he wasn't, but—"

"No buts. Every guy that's showed an interest in you has gotten the cold shoulder. I understood at first because Seth had come on strong, but now—"

"Now's no different." She ran a hand over her bound hair and moaned.

"Seth's a grown man. He's been married and he's been hurt. After his accident he was a little off balance, but who wouldn't be considering the circumstances?"

She closed her eyes and slowly shook her head back and forth. "Jake, you don't need to explain Seth to me, but you've got to realize *if* Seth's interested in me, it's *gratitude* and nothing more. Which is exactly what I told him when he brought it up."

Jake's eyes widened and she hated the gleam she'd inadvertently put there by admitting she and Seth had talked about a…relationship. "Get that look off your face," she ordered. "Seth is a good man, Jake. He's kind and sweet and gentle but—"

Jake burst out laughing. *"Sweet?"*

She belted him on the arm.

"Ow! Okay, sweet. Whatever."

"And he's a patient."

"But he won't be a patient forever, and what's your excuse going to be then?"

She groaned. "You sound like Seth." She rubbed her temple and shot him an irritated look. "You know you should be helping me instead of encouraging this."

Jake tugged her close again, his arm loose atop her shoulders.

"You left Seth because things were getting too serious, too fast. I respected your decision, but now…Grace, you can't be afraid of tying yourself to someone."

"Who says I am?"

Jake's face revealed his thoughts. "Seth won't hurt you."

The few times Jake had tried to talk to her in high school about the bruises he saw on her wrists, she'd cut him off and threatened not to be his friend. And although he'd held his questions and his temper, she knew Jake had noticed the bruises had stopped when Earl died.

"Everything okay?" Maura asked as she walked toward them.

Jake flashed his wife a smile and a nod as he lifted his other arm for Maura to slide under. As if she sensed the emotions of the moment, Maura initiated a group hug, her gaze sympathetic as she studied Grace.

"If you're thinking about leaving, please, Grace,

don't," Maura begged. "I don't know what we'd do without you."

"Can anyone join in this?"

Seth. Grace stiffened, and by the looks on Jake's and Maura's faces when she pulled away, she realized they were both aware of her turbulent feelings for him. Did everyone know? Did Seth?

"I've got two beautiful women in my arms and you show up?" Jake sighed. "All right, you can have one," he said as he gently shoved her away.

Grace stumbled, her eyes wide that Jake would dare say, much less *do,* such a thing, only to find herself tripping over Seth's feet and landing on his lap. His arms wrapped around her, steadying her, and all of a sudden, she and Seth were alone on the road because Jake had swung Maura up into his arms and began walking away.

"Sorry, guys, urgent news just in. Lexi's spending the day at a friend's house so—" His eyebrows went up and down a couple of times and Maura's laughter filled the air as Jake's strides carried her quickly toward the house.

Grace stared after them, realized she was sitting there in Seth's lap unmoving, and attempted to leap to her feet.

"I don't bite," he said, his tone urging her to stay. "What were you and Jake discussing that had you looking so upset?"

She shook her head. "Let me up."

"Tonight if you can't sleep, why don't we go for a walk? We can bundle up and go sit by the stream. Might be the last of our good weather."

The breeze rustled the dried leaves all around them and brought Seth's masculine scent to her nose. Spice and citrus. Cologne? That was new. Another little way he proved to be getting better every day.

"Well?" he murmured.

She nodded once, wetting her lips when she noticed Seth staring at her mouth. He raised a callused hand and tucked a stray curl behind her ear. His knuckles were gentle as they brushed her cheek. Effortlessly, he brought her lips to his.

Warm and musky, Seth's kiss made her forget all about their surroundings. Forget the warnings in her head. Forget everything but the security of his arms, the gentleness of his touch.

One palm cradled her face while the other simply supported her back where she sat on his lap. He didn't rush her, didn't push for anything more than a kiss.

And, oh, what a kiss it was.

She shifted sideways to attain a more comfortable position, bracing her forearms on his shoulders. Their kiss deepened, fierce in its intensity, then Seth pulled back, nose to nose, his gaze on hers as if to check to make sure she was okay.

When she didn't protest, didn't move, his mouth snagged hers again. And again. He kissed her over and over, from every angle. Sweet and gentle, deep and sensual. No kiss was ever the same. And she'd never enjoyed anything more. Just kissing. His hands caressed her spine, but he made no move to touch her anywhere else. After a long, long while Seth eased her away, his ragged breathing matching hers.

Her lips tingled, her lower body ached in an unfamiliar way, but she wasn't so naive she didn't recognize the signs.

Desire. He'd made her want more. Want *him*.

Made her feel sexy and sensual. Not dirty.

Stunned by her emotions, Grace pulled away, tasting Seth in her mouth. And while she wanted to press her lips back to his, to see if the feelings would still be the same, she needed time to think, to cope. To come to a decision.

Seth let her go without comment, and she stood, the cold air chilling her. She wrapped her arms around her middle for warmth and began walking back to the house, Seth wheeling himself along at her side.

CHAPTER TWELVE

PROGRESS WAS A POWERFUL rush, Seth thought days later. Especially when that progress came in the form of Grace's acceptance of him. He touched her as much as possible during therapy, since it was their main time alone together during the day. Light, teasing caresses to her arm or shoulder. A hand at her waist or hip.

He wanted her. He wanted her smile and gentleness. Her beauty and strength. He wanted all of her. Even her past.

Seth pushed open the door to the den and found Jake inside. His brother looked up, then sat back in the desk chair and grinned at him, looking much like Lexi's kitten when he saw a full bowl of cream that was his and his alone.

Jake whistled, shaking his head slowly back and forth.

"What?" he growled, not sure he was in the mood for Jake's teasing. Not when his nerves were strung tight from being so close to Grace and yet not close enough. It took every ounce of energy not to rush her, push too hard. Or worry that if she did accept him and want to make love, he wouldn't be able to follow through with the act. Getting it up was no problem, but what if he couldn't *keep* it up?

His brother's smile widened. "I still can't believe the difference." Jake chuckled. "I'm not complaining, it's going to take some getting used to is all." He tossed the pen he held onto the papers in front of him. "What's up?"

Seth frowned. "What do you know about Earl Korbit? He was already dead when Grace and I dated, but you knew her before."

Jake leaned an elbow on the arm of his chair and rubbed his jaw. "I know he used to beat up on them. Are you wondering why I didn't say something?"

Seth rolled himself over to the desk and picked up the horseshoe puzzle sitting on the corner. "You were her best friend."

"I still am," Jake corrected with a glare. "I've always stood by her, and before you scowl at me it was never like *that*." Jake leaned back and teased him with another grin. "And if my own wife trusts me in that department, I certainly hope my brother does. Grace was…different. Tough as nails on the outside, but fragile on the inside."

"That hasn't changed."

"Earl's abuse took a toll," Jake agreed.

Seth shook the metal pieces, frustrated he couldn't work the puzzle as quickly as in the past. "So why didn't you say anything?"

"Who says I didn't?"

Seth looked up when he heard the tension lining Jake's voice, the puzzle forgotten.

"I skipped out of school one day and went to the sheriff."

"How bad was she?" he asked, his voice hoarse from fury.

Jake's expression darkened. "Black eye, fat lip, bruises on her arms, her neck. She tried to hide them with a turtleneck, and maybe for the teachers her excuses were enough, but not for me. I was sick of it and I told the sheriff what was going on." His laugh lacked all traces of humor. "He took me into his office and sat me down and said, 'Listen up, boy. We don't have a system for that here, so if you tell me I have to do something about a man *disciplining* his children, you ought to know what'll happen to them.'"

Jake ran a hand through his hair, swearing under his breath. "He went on to tell me every horror story he'd heard about foster care and state institutions for troubled or abandoned kids. How pretty girls were quickly accepted into homes because—" A muscle ticked in his jaw. "I couldn't do it, Seth. I was more afraid of what would happen to her there than what was happening at home. Earl hit them when he was drunk, but Brent told me more than once the rest of the time Earl was…decent. Which was a sight better than what she could've faced in one of the homes at the hands of some pervert."

Seth nodded and tried to ignore the anger eating away at his soul at what Grace had endured, reminding himself Jake didn't know how bad it had actually been. Unless Grace made her secret public, it would die with him.

Seth swung his wheelchair around.

"Seth, wait." Jake's stare was hard on his. "I know what you're trying to do with the studio. Grace probably told you Maura is upset and wanting a place of our own so you offered, but I don't want it. I want nothing that was hers."

Seth stared at him, wishing for the millionth time he and Jake could find some common ground where Arie was concerned.

"Jake—"

"The house is fine. Maura will get over it as soon as her hormones calm down. We've lived here with Lex since she was born, we can stay for the baby. I want nothing to do with the cabin, not when the place reminds me so much of Arie."

"You can't blame Maura for wanting a home of her own."

"But I'll never be able to live in the studio and

not think about what happened. Or what could've happened. Her stuff can be removed, but the memory will always be there. The thought alone makes me want to—" Jake broke off with a curse. "I know you loved her, Seth, but that's how I feel."

Seth swung himself around and headed for the door before he said something he shouldn't. Jake had every right to be angry. They all did. But he also thought Maura ought to know the truth.

"Seth?"

He paused, his hand on the knob.

"Take it slow with Grace. It's obvious she still cares for you, but her past with Earl…it's all inside her. Don't go too fast and give her an excuse to push you away again."

THEIR MIDNIGHT RENDEZVOUS became the norm. Sometimes she and Seth would sit and talk in front of the fire, or go outside into the cold, crisp air to walk around the ranch. But since that day Jake pushed her onto Seth's lap, they hadn't kissed. And now as Thanksgiving had passed and Christmas drew near, she found herself looking forward to their private time together more and more. And wanting things she shouldn't want.

Since telling Seth about Earl's abuse, she was more comfortable with him than she had been with any other person in her life. She only wished he'd open up to her about his wife and address the tension Arie's name created whenever she attempted to bring up their marriage.

Grace was sitting in the living room when she heard the push-whirl of Seth's wheelchair on the hardwood floors. He'd gained weight, strength and muscle mass, and was able to get himself in and out of bed without help. Since putting his mind to the task, his therapy had advanced better than she could've hoped and soon he wouldn't need her any longer.

So what would she do when it was time to leave? She groaned softly and stuck her fingers into her hair to push it out of her face.

"I know what you're thinking," Seth said from behind her.

Her eyes widened and she swallowed as she looked over her shoulder. "Oh? And what's that?"

"You're plotting how to torture me next."

She laughed, relieved that her thoughts weren't that easy to interpret. "Got that right. Tomorrow we begin water therapy. It's about time you put that whirlpool to work."

His mouth curved up in a sinful grin. "Will you join me?"

She glanced at him and thanked the darkness for hiding her flaming cheeks. The flirtatious question hung in the air between them and her heartbeat accelerated.

"We'll, uh, see," she whispered, unable to help herself. It wasn't unheard of for a PT to get into the whirlpool with a patient, especially if the patient was bigger and maneuvering him posed a potential problem. But getting in the whirlpool with Seth? Bad idea. Bad, bad, bad.

"I talked to your brother tonight. Brent called after you went to your room. I would've come to get you, but I hoped you were sleeping and I didn't want to disturb you. He said to tell you he aced the final he was worried about and he'd call tomorrow."

"I'm sorry I missed him." Grace turned to more fully face him, curling her legs up in the chair. "You know…you don't need to keep me company. I appreciate what you've done these past few weeks but…"

"But what?" Seth's inquisitive eyes were tender and compelling. "Trying to get rid of me?"

She looped her arms around her legs and hugged her knees to her chest. "Of course not, it's just—"

Seth pushed himself closer, right up to the edge of the wing chair where she sat. With her legs drawn up out of the way, he didn't stop until the front of his calves hit the cushioned leather. He leaned forward, holding her gaze as the air around them stilled.

"Just what? Are you afraid of me, Grace?"

She blew her breath out in a rush. "No," she whispered firmly. "No, I'm not afraid of you." *Terrified* was more like it.

"Does my chair bother you?"

"No."

He bothered her. Made her unsatisfied with her life, because after staying with Seth she realized she wanted more, wanted to stop traveling all over the country and put down roots. She wanted—she wanted—

"Good. Because I want to talk to you about us."

Scared witless, Grace unwrapped her arms from about her legs and pushed his wheelchair away from her seat far enough to swing her feet to the floor. She stood, intending to walk by him to go to the kitchen, but he snagged her hand and wouldn't let go.

"Seth, please," she begged, even though her body followed his urging to sit down again.

"I've been thinking a lot about you and what you've been through. I've been patient. Made sure I didn't do anything to scare you. I haven't, have I?"

The note of insecurity in his tone cut deep. He'd been more than patient. More than tender. "Yes, you have and I—"

"I'm getting better every day."

She nodded hesitantly, agreeing. Did he want her to leave now? Was this his way of getting rid of her? Maybe that's why he hadn't kissed her.

"But it struck me today…really struck me…that

you're not afraid of me, the patient, but me, the man. Because you haven't been with anyone since Earl's abuse." He paused. "Have you?"

She wished the floor would open up and swallow her whole. Did she really want Seth to know everything? "No."

He blinked once. "No? No, back off and leave you alone, or no, you haven't been with anyone else?"

She closed her eyes, her body so hot she'd surely melt. It was none of his business. None. "No... I haven't. I tried. W-With you and—and someone else, but...I couldn't."

Seth reached for one of her hands and brought her fingers to his mouth. He kissed them gently, one by one, and she shifted against the leather cushion and tried to ignore the touch of his tongue.

"Seth, we had a past, but ethically—"

"Look at me, Grace."

It took her a moment. A long, drawn out, I-can't-do-this moment, before she raised her gaze to his. Holding it was another battle all together, but she managed that, too.

"I'm not some young fool in heat like I was when we dated. We've talked about everything under the sun. Shared things we've *never* told anyone else," he pressed. "But this—*us*—boils down to whether or not I'm only a patient to you…and whether or not you think you can love me the way I—"

"You *are* a patient," she hissed, looking away when she panicked and couldn't handle the intensity any longer. She was lying and they both knew it.

Seth tugged her forward in the chair, and off balance, her breath left her lungs. She watched, everything happening so fast yet in slow motion as his free hand lifted to cradle her face. She relished the warmth of his callused skin against her cold cheek, the gentleness he showed her when she expected—*expected*—brutality.

Was he really going to say he loved her?

Then he kissed her, startling her out of her turbulent thoughts. Still feeling more than a bit out of body, she was conscious of his thumbs stroking her cheekbones, adding to the dizzying, terrifying sensations buffeting her.

"Easy, Grace. That's it. Come sit on my lap."

She whimpered softly and shook her head. Fearful, lost.

Remembering.

"Listen to my voice, sweetheart. It's all right. Let me hold you, Grace. I won't hurt you. I'll never hurt you."

Seth's voice collided with Earl's in her head, battled, as he placed brief, tantalizing kisses on her mouth. Tempted her to open her lips and nudge her tongue to his.

"I won't hurt you, honey. I'd never deliberately hurt you. Trust me…please, Grace, trust me."

His mouth caught hers in another heady kiss, stole her breath and numbed her senses to the fact he scooped her off the chair and onto his lap with little effort. He was strong now, getting stronger, but she wasn't frightened of his strength. *Because this was Seth.*

One kiss blended into two, two into a dozen, as Seth continued to hold her, rub her back and ease the tension lining her shoulders and neck.

She pulled away, wanting to initiate a kiss, but still unsure. His dark lashes rose lazily, his eyes hot and needy, but he gave her the space and time she required to follow through with her thoughts.

Grace licked her lips and his gaze dropped to her mouth, the look in his eyes—it should have scared her but it didn't. The look filled her with power, security. Love?

She ran her fingers over his lips. Soft yet firm. Seth's touch wasn't about pain or rape or domination. And the undeniable relief brought by the thought had her lowering her mouth to his for a kiss entirely her own to give.

His lips parted as she bent toward him and she smiled slightly, teasing. And like she'd known he would, Seth merely waited patiently for her. He didn't press her or force the kiss, passing her last and final test with ease.

In response to his gift, she took his lower lip into her mouth and nibbled before she sucked the flesh as he'd done to her. Seth muttered her name, and the rough sound sent shivers through her. She slipped her hand down Seth's shoulder, lingered on the thick bulge of muscle in his upper arms before finding his broad hand. She squeezed once before lifting it to her breast, and Seth stilled, his entire body taut.

She didn't open her eyes. Grace kept her mouth glued to his while she waited to see what he would do. While *she* waited for the panic to come and overwhelm her. This time the test was for them both. Her heart raced, her breathing turned choppy, but then both those things had occurred before she'd pressed his hand there. She wasn't sick or nauseous. She was…okay.

She squeezed his hand again, urging him to touch her, and Seth's fingers flexed against her through the cloth of her robe and pajamas, gentle and firm as his thumb found her, circled, the tip of his nail rasping against the peak. "Ah, honey, this is how it's supposed to be. So good and sweet. I don't want to frighten you," he muttered hoarsely. "Tell me if I—"

"Yes," she said, biting her lip to hold back a

gasp when his hand slipped beneath the robe, her pajama top.

"Tell me no and I'll stop. Don't be afraid. Don't ever be afraid of me." Seth's hand caressed its way up her body. The soft curve of her stomach, the shape of her ribs. By the time he made it to her breast, Grace held her breath in anticipation...and fear. What if she panicked again?

He'd stop.

But what if—

Seth's fingers found the tip, lightly pinched, and her lips parted in a hiss as she sucked in more air.

"Beautiful," he whispered huskily. "You are so beautiful." One of his large, callused hands teased its way up and down her spine while his other hand caressed her. "Grace, we have to stop. You're not ready for more, sweetheart. You know you're not." He pressed a kiss to the skin above her breast, directly over her heart. "We have to stop," he said again, as though trying to convince himself and not just her.

He pressed his mouth to her hair, her forehead. Chaste, tender kisses that didn't do anything to curb the heat burning inside her, or stop her thoughts from returning to the darkness within, to the place where doubts and fears abounded.

She hadn't panicked this time, but then, they hadn't made love, either.

SETH STARED AT GRACE and frowned. She wouldn't look at him, barely talked to him over breakfast. Now it was nearly lunchtime and the silence was getting to him. Whatever she worried about had to be addressed. He was debating how to broach the subject when Lexi ran into the room, a book clutched in her arms and Blackie, the all-white kitten, scampering behind her.

"Uncle Seff! Look what Daddy brought me." Without hesitation she climbed up on his lap and Seth dropped the free weights he held to help her. "A picture book 'bout Christmas! Can we go to the parade tonight? Please? Daddy has to work 'n' Mommy don't feel like going. Will you go 'n' take me?"

The change of topics occurred so fast Seth blinked at the blue eyes looking up at him. He tugged on one of her pigtails. "We'll go if Grace will take us," he said, plenty loud enough for Grace to hear. "We'll make a date of it. The three of us."

Grace spun around. Her mouth opening and snapping shut twice before she got any words out. "A…date?"

"Yay!" Lexi cried, grinning. "Uncle Seff 'n' Grace sittin' in a tree—"

"Lexi—"

"K-i-s-s-i—"

"All right, you, enough of that," Seth said, his gaze on Grace's horrified expression. "We made our point," he whispered to Lexi conspiratorially, winking. "Let me finish my therapy and then we'll eat lunch together. Okay?"

"Can I stay?"

"No, honey, right now it might be best for you to scoot. Go see if Maura will read your book to you."

For once his niece complied without complaint. Lexi climbed down from his lap, retrieved her book from the floor where it had slid in the process, and skipped over to Grace. She wrapped her little arms around Grace's legs.

"Thank you, Grace."

Grace fingered the curly end of a braided pigtail. "For what?"

"Makin' Uncle Seff happy again."

Seth flashed Grace a knowing smile as he bent and picked up the weights he'd dropped. Grace *had* made him happy. In more ways than one. She'd fought with him and given him back his will to belong in the world—whether he recovered or not.

Grace watched Lexi skip from the room, sparing him a glare before she went back to checking the temperature in the whirlpool. "We are not going on a *date*."

He finished his lifts, did a couple of extra because he now could, and then dropped the barbells again before wheeling himself over to where she stood. "Yes, we are. Tonight's the Holly Days Parade in town and I don't want to miss it."

"Hank can take you," she murmured, her face averted.

"Hank'll be taking his own family. I want you." He paused deliberately before adding, "To take us."

Grace clearly knew what he meant. Her face revealed her panic. "Seth, you know as well as I do that last night was a mistake. I was wrong to let it happen."

"So why did you?"

"Because…I guess because I wanted to know…" She shook her head and waved a hand in the air before stalking across the room. She grabbed a clipboard from the countertop and made a notation. "Y-You've helped me with my nightmares tremendously, but our little…experimentation doesn't change the fact I'm your therapist and I'll be leaving soon."

"That wasn't the question. What did you want to know? If you were beautiful? Womanly? If you could feel passion without fear?"

He knew he'd gotten it right when she stilled.

"It wasn't just an experiment, Grace. You are a woman through and through. Now go with me tonight. Lexi will chaperone us." He rolled himself across the room and ran a knuckle down her bare arm, pleased when a shiver racked her. "I can't do much in front of a five-year-old, now can I? Come on, Grace. Don't make me face them alone."

It was a low blow, but he wasn't above using every advantage. Grace knew he hadn't been in town since the accident. It had been one of his midnight confessions. Facing his friends and neighbors again wasn't going to be easy. For his first trip he definitely wanted Grace by his side. Wanted her to have fun with him and Lex. Picture herself beside him for the rest of her life.

"That's not fair. And while it's easy to say it doesn't matter, I do have a reputation to think of. Yes, we have a past and you're not my typical patient," she admitted, "but what if word gets out that I'm on a date with you?"

Seth nodded, absurdly pleased she'd said the word even as she balked. He thought for a moment, then picked her hand up and brought it to his mouth. "I'll take care of it."

"How?"

"By firing you," he said calmly, "until tomorrow morning's therapy session. See? Problem solved."

She groaned, the sound weary. "Seth—"

"Getting Jake to back me up won't be a problem. Hey, Jake!"

"Seth, no!"

"Jake!"

"Shh," she ordered, a smile on her lips. "Okay, okay, hush! Just hush or Jake'll never let me live it down."

"You'll go?"

She released a resigned sigh. "Yes, but get back to work. You're going to pay for blackmailing me."

CHAPTER THIRTEEN

LATER THAT EVENING Grace rolled her eyes and sighed. "This is crazy," she murmured to herself, yanking off the slacks—in an attempt to find something appropriate for her date with Seth. "It's not a *date*."

She pulled a long black dress from her closet and held it up in front of her, staring at herself in the mirror. She'd bought the classic A-line dress for a funeral and considering she'd spent the last ten years in baggy, figure-hiding clothes, her options were limited. Her nights were usually spent catching up on laundry, reading or exercising. Anything and everything that didn't cost money considering Brent's tuition bills were always right around the corner.

Her brother didn't like accepting money from her, and had made her promise he could pay her back once he graduated, but until then…she did what she could to keep him from graduating college over his head in debt.

However, tonight was the one night a year the little town of North Star pulled out all the stops in celebrating Christmas, and she wouldn't mind having a look around to see how things had changed since she'd been gone. And she needed the right outfit to give her confidence.

"It's *not* a *date,*" she repeated, glaring at herself in the mirror. She turned around, threw the dress on the bed until she found the hem and scrunched it up to pull it over her head, twisting and squirming until she got the back zipper zipped. No matter what she looked like, this was it. She refused to change again. She tackled her hair next, pulling it up in a sloppy twist before curling her long bangs until they framed her jaw.

"Grace, you ready?"

She jumped at the sound of Seth's voice, then stuck her tongue out at herself in the mirror. Hands shaking, she spritzed on some hairspray, added a touch of lipstick to her lips, then smoothed her hands over her stomach and hips before glaring at herself again.

"Grace?"

She whirled around, left the bathroom and headed for the door between their rooms. She yanked it open and walked into Seth's room, only to stop in her tracks.

Seth was bare from the waist up.

"Oh, I—the way you were bellowing I thought you were ready."

"No problem," he drawled, his tone full of amusement. "Could you get a nice shirt from my closet? Maura's already ironed a couple and hung them up, but the bar's too high. Pick your favorite."

Her favorite? Grace hurried to the open closet. She grabbed the first shirt that came to hand, but then hesitated and discreetly chose another, one that would bring out Seth's dark complexion and beautiful eyes.

She winced at the thought and turned, surprised he'd moved closer to where she stood without her hearing. Had he seen what she'd done?

Face heating, her gaze dropped. He'd regained the weight lost since the accident and filled out nicely. His shoulders were broad, his arms delineated from lifting weights. His chest muscular and lightly covered with dark curls that tapered down to his abdomen and disappeared into his jeans.

"Grace?"

"What?" Only then did she realize she'd been standing there and staring at him. No, not staring. *Gawking.* And Seth had noticed.

A seductive smile hovered at the corners of his mouth and it was obvious he enjoyed that she couldn't take her eyes off him.

"The shirt?"

She glanced down at the material now wadded in her clenched fingers and hurriedly tossed the shirt at him, forcing him to lunge to catch it before it hit him in the face. He chuckled. "Thanks, darlin'."

"I'm not your *darlin'* and this is not a date," she argued.

"I heard you the first time." He leaned sideways in the chair to pull the shirt on, a spark of mischievousness in his eyes. "And every other time you told yourself that in your room," he added, amusement giving his words a lilt.

He'd heard her talking to herself? She chose to ignore the taunt and stalked across the floor. "I'm going to go check on Lexi."

"I'm glad you like what you see, Grace, and for the record, I do, too. I can't wait until I get my goodnight kiss tonight. You know, when we end our date."

"It's not a *date!*"

His knee-weakening laugh followed her from the room.

SETH LEANED BACK AGAINST the bucket seat of the extended-cab truck and smiled. Grace's face was lit with a grin much like his niece's, and between the two of them, he wasn't quite sure who was more excited watching the parade amble by.

Horns honked, and elves dressed in green sweats and silly hats with bells on the pointy ends passed out candy canes. The high school band marched by, and the crowd began cheering loudly, a sure sign Santa Claus had been sighted farther down the street.

"I can't see him!" Lexi complained. Grace picked Lex up and settled her on her hip, the move as natural as any mother's.

The band began playing "Here Comes Santa Claus" and Lexi shouted, "There he is! I see him!"

Grace glanced over her shoulder at Seth, then quickly turned back to face the street. She'd been doing that all night, giving him those quick, intense stares ever since he'd revealed the fact that he'd heard her talking to herself in her bedroom. And that he intended to snag another kiss before the night was over.

He smiled. Slow and steady wins the race, he mused, quoting his father's favorite saying. Even though the word *date* apparently sent pure terror through her, Grace hadn't actually protested all that much.

The noise level grew as the fire truck crawled by them with Santa waving and yelling out "Ho, Ho, Ho!" Once he passed, the crowd quickly scattered, most everyone falling into step behind the slow-moving vehicle for the walk to Main Street.

Santa led the way to the church located in the town square, and there, the man in red doffed his hat and knelt before the live manger scene. After a short play where the Wise Men presented their gifts, the Christmas tree was officially lit and the church opened its doors for coffee, cider and cookies.

Grace and Lexi got back into the truck with Seth, strapped themselves in, and Grace pulled the truck out onto the busy street to follow the crowd. All without comment.

"You have to talk to me sometime," he murmured.

"No, I don't," she countered quickly, and then winced when he laughed because she'd broken her silence for the sake of arguing.

Seth sighed and propped his hand on the seat near her head. "What do you want for Christmas?"

She shook her head back and forth, carefully easing the truck along the street at a snail's pace so as not to get too close to the crowd. "Nothing. You don't have to get me anything."

"I want a doll and a baby crib and a—"

Grace laughed softly as she slid a glance over her shoulder to Lexi. "Sounds like you need to write a letter to Santa."

"Uh-uh," Lexi corrected. "I'm gonna send an e-mail. He'll get it faster."

They both chuckled at Lexi's response, but Seth's gaze never left Grace's full lips and amused expression. Grace loved his niece, and even though it shouldn't surprise him, at odd moments it did.

"Grace, hurry! We're gonna miss everything!"

"Okay, okay!" Grace laughed, then furtively glanced his way. He winked at her, then smiled when her lips parted in a gasp.

She was so easy to play with, so responsive to a look or a touch. A kiss. He closed his eyes and remembered her in his arms last night, how she'd moaned and sighed and arched into his touch once she'd pushed aside her fears.

Grace signaled and headed down an alley.

"There's an opening right there." Seth pointed toward an empty spot. Grace parked the truck, then picked up the handicapped tag and placed it on the mirror.

"Look out there, Grace."

She took in the bright, twinkling lights, the people walking and laughing. The couples, young and old, holding hands.

"Just so we're clear," he murmured softly, leaning near her so Lexi couldn't overhear. "I want that with you. We had something close once, but this time I want more. I want everything. Take as much time as you need, but don't think for a second I'm going to let you run away again because of what happened." He smoothed his hand over her hair. "I want all of you. *Especially* your past. Because it made you the person you are right now."

"Are you kissin'? Come on, Uncle Seff, hurry! Let's go before Santa leaves!"

"I WANT ALL OF YOU... Especially your past."

The words echoed in Grace's mind over and over as the Christmas skit ended. She bowed her head as the prayer was said and Santa stepped forward to take his place for pictures. Lexi squirmed in her arms and wanted to join the throng of kids rushing the poor man, but Grace kept to the back of the crowd and waited patiently while most of the parents retrieved their kids and formed a sprawling line.

"Uncle Seff's talkin' too long, Grace. I gotta tell Santa what I want since he's here. Please?"

Grace looked over at Seth and found him surrounded by men, laughing and talking, at ease for the time being. "Well...he does seem to be holding his own, so I guess it wouldn't hurt."

"I'm glad you're dating us."

Grace pointedly ignored the child's comment and lowered Lexi to her side, capturing the little girl's hand before she could take off through the crowd.

"Better stay close, Lex. You wouldn't want Grace to lose you again."

Grace stiffened at the sound of Roy Bernard's voice and turned to find the ranch hand standing nearby, his gaze sliding over her with indecent thoroughness. Grace's hand tightened on Lexi's when the child tried to pull loose, and Bernard noted the movement, a smile twisting his mouth.

"Here, I got you something," he said as he held a gift bag out to Lexi. Before Grace could stop her, Jake's daughter grabbed the bag and yanked free of her hold to stick her hand inside. She pulled out a fragile-looking doll.

"Oh, thank you, Roy!" Lexi pulled the doll to her chest and danced in place. "She's so pretty!"

Grace hesitated. "Lexi, I don't know that you should accept her. She looks very…expensive."

"It's a Christmas present," Roy gritted out, his voice low. "She's been talkin' about wantin' a fancy doll the last couple months."

"Then maybe Santa or her parents would've brought her one." She glanced down and put her hand on Lexi's shoulder. "I can tell you like her, but I think you should give the doll back to Roy."

Roy stepped closer to her, and even though she was surrounded by a crowd of jovial people, Grace knew a threat when she saw one. It took everything in her not to give in to her impulse and back up a step.

"Earl said you liked to talk back. Told me how he'd punish you. Now be nice to me or else we'll have one of those *talks* like you and Earl used to have," he growled, his voice too low to be overheard by anyone else.

Dizzy, shocked, Grace stared at him in horror until Roy turned on his heel and stalked away, disappearing into the crowd before she could form a response.

"There're my girls," Seth said, joining them. "Let's go inside where it's warm."

Grace looked down at Lexi and found her petting the doll's curly hair and talking to it, holding it as if the gift were precious. Shaken, disbelieving, she bent and grabbed the empty bag at Lexi's feet.

"What's that?" Seth asked.

Lexi clutched the doll closer. "I want to keep her. She's mine!"

Grace looked to Seth, unable and unwilling to keep quiet. No matter what Roy threatened. "Roy was here. He gave Lexi a doll for Christmas, but I told her she should give it back."

Seth ran a gloved hand over his face. "Grace is right, Lex. It doesn't look cheap and he doesn't get paid enough the way it is."

"*No!*" Lexi stomped a foot. "She's mine. He *gave* her to me."

Grace cleared her throat. "He—Roy said some things to me, too," she continued, unable to look at him. "Threatening things."

Seth reached for her hand. "What'd he say? Are you all right?"

"Can I keep her? Please, Uncle Seff, please?" Lexi whimpered.

Grace nodded, accepting the hand he laid on hers

and squeezing his fingers. "We can talk later," she murmured, knowing neither she nor Seth would let Roy get anywhere near her the rest of the night.

Seth pointed to the open doors of the reception hall. "Let's go in and warm up. Maybe we can talk in there."

Apparently trying to gain favor by behaving, Lexi forgot about talking to Santa all together and quietly followed her uncle as Seth led the way into the church. He snagged an empty spot in a far corner where his chair wouldn't block the walkway and tried to get Grace to sit with him and tell him what happened with Roy, but Lexi's demand for cookies couldn't be ignored.

Plus Grace didn't want to discuss Roy in such a public setting, where someone might overhear, so she used Lexi as an excuse to avoid the topic for the moment.

Grace grabbed a couple of cookies and a cup of hot chocolate for Lexi, and tried to put the incident behind her. She wanted to enjoy her time with Seth while she had the chance.

She prodded Lexi forward through the thickening crowd and into the corner where Seth now sat surrounded. Lexi darted her way through the people and climbed up to sit on her uncle's lap, and Grace's heart lurched at the sight.

Seth was so dark and handsome, whereas Lexi

was angelic-looking and pale. If what everyone said was true, she could only imagine how gorgeous Arie must have been in person, and what a striking couple she and Seth must have made. Jealousy stabbed her before she could suppress it.

Chin up, Grace hesitantly made her way to the table to set the treats in front of Seth's niece. She'd turned to step away when Seth caught her hand.

She bent, her voice low as she warned, "You're going to start the gossip mills. Did you need something?"

"Just you." He chuckled softly. "No, don't run off. Stay with me. Please, Grace."

Her cheeks flushed with warmth when the man beside Seth grinned. "Well now, I can certainly see why you'd want her to stay. Introduce us, Seth. Or I guess I should say, reintroduce us."

Seth winked at her again and squeezed her hand in encouragement. "Grace, Phil Estes. He graduated a year behind you and Jake. Phil, Grace Korbit. Mind your manners, Phil."

The heat in her cheeks deepened. Seth's possessive tone was unmistakable, and if she sensed it, she figured everyone around them did, too. "Nice to see you, Phil," she said, holding out her free hand. Phil grasped her fingers in his and gave them a hearty shake, returning the greeting.

"Well, now, of all the things to get through to

Seth and make him come to his senses, I'd say you've done it."

She laughed awkwardly. "You're giving me way too much credit. Seth got tired of me yelling at him and decided getting better is the only way to get rid of me. That's all."

"If you say so." The man paused long enough to take a sip of coffee, then muttered something under his breath. "Hey, Seth, I almost forgot. Jake called me a while ago. Said if I saw you to tell you that you might want to head home soon."

Grace glanced at Seth and frowned. "Do you think Maura's okay?"

Seth nodded. "I'm sure it's nothing major, but maybe we'd better go." He offered Phil his hand. "Been nice talking to you. Come see me this week. We need to work on some things. Important things."

"Will do." Phil slapped Seth on the shoulder. "It's good to see you out again. Take care."

"Do we gotta go home?"

"Yes," Seth answered, his tone firm. "No arguing."

"Will you ride me to the truck?"

Seth told Lexi to hold on as he backed up and performed a wheelie, causing his audience to smile and laugh at Lexi's squeal of delight. Smiling herself, Grace murmured a general goodbye and followed Seth and Lexi out the door.

In the truck, Lexi sang "Jingle Bells" over and over and eased the strain of having to make conversation with Seth. Before Grace knew it, she'd turned down the ranch's long driveway. In a matter of moments, their "date" would be over, and it would be time for the good-night kiss.

"Can we go to the cabin? We haven't been there forever," Lexi pleaded. "Please, Uncle Seff? Please?"

"We need to get home, Lex."

"But what about our present for Mommy and Daddy?"

Grace glanced at Seth and saw him sigh. "I guess we do need to get it, don't we? Christmas is coming up fast. But we can't stay long, Lex. It's past your bedtime. We'll get the picture and leave, got it?"

Grace heard a forlorn agreement from the back seat and eased off the gas as she turned up the drive to the cabin. They hit a couple of shallow holes and the truck rocked. She pulled up to the tiny, picturesque cabin and shivered as she remembered the night Roy had found her alone.

His comments tonight were equally frightening, and she knew she had to do something about him, but what? If Roy suspected anything about her past, if he really knew how Earl had "disciplined" her, it was possible others did, too.

No one knows. Roy's playing on your fears. He only knows Earl hit you, so what?

That had to be it. But if not, how would she face people? It was stupid and childish, and even though she knew Earl's abuse wasn't her fault, she was embarrassed and ashamed. Seth was such a good man, had always been popular in the small community. How would it look if the truth got out about her? She didn't want to do anything, *be* someone, who'd make Seth look bad. Especially not when he was finally getting his life back. She couldn't do that to him. Not when she cared for him enough to want better for him.

"Let's go!" Lexi cried impatiently.

"All right," Seth muttered with a laugh. "Give me a second to get situated."

He lifted his chair from behind his seat, dropped it to the ground outside, and made the transfer with ease. Lexi hopped out after him and ran to the door while Grace lagged behind, hugging herself for warmth.

The door squeaked open without the benefit of the flower-pot's key, but before she could comment on that, Grace saw Seth trying to maneuver the single step leading inside. She rushed forward and grabbed the handles of his chair, giving him the extra balance to make the shift up.

"Thanks."

She nodded dazedly, wincing when Lexi flipped a switch and light flooded the cabin.

The child grinned from ear to ear. "See? I told you Aunt Arie liked to paint."

Grace forced a smile, inordinately glad she'd been prepared for this moment. "I can see that. They're very beautiful." She walked over to stare at the charcoal drawing of Seth in chaps and a Stetson. Drawn to it much as she'd been the first time she'd seen it. "Your aunt was quite talented."

Seth scowled. "Yeah, she was something else," he agreed, his tone low and…reverent?

Yes, she decided. Most definitely reverent. Grace glanced at Seth and found him fingering a paint-brush, his face drawn in pain-filled lines of sorrow.

"When I grow up I want to be just like her," Lexi stated. "An artist."

A muscle twitched in Seth's jaw, his face a mask of grief before he tossed his head in an angry jerk and headed to the back of the cabin.

"Five minutes," he said gruffly over his shoulder. "Then we leave. I'll get the picture."

The little girl scampered up the stairs without knocking or bumping the many paintings, and Grace shifted from foot to foot, painfully uncomfortable witnessing Seth's obvious distress.

What could she possibly offer Seth? A truckload of emotional baggage? A random fear of the dark?

Nightmares? Seth deserved better. More than she could ever give him being who she was.

Lexi peered over the banister. "Somebody's been here. The bed's messed up."

Seth frowned. "The painting isn't where it used to be, either. Get down here, Lex. Now. It's time to go, anyway."

The little girl stuck her lip out in a pout but did as she was told, and Grace watched her to make sure she managed the narrow staircase without falling.

"Want me to go look?" she asked hesitantly.

Seth rubbed a hand over his face and shrugged. "Yeah. The painting is of Lexi. It's a big one. Lexi is wearing wings like an angel."

She knew exactly which painting but couldn't say or else let it be known she'd been there before. Grace slowly climbed the stairs, but paused at the top. The bed had indeed been slept in, the covers hanging off the side and the pillow indented. Maura must have come to the cabin to get away, since she hadn't had any luck convincing Jake to move in now that they'd gotten permission from Seth.

She carefully removed the painting of Lexi from the wall, and the act put her face-to-face with Arie's talent. With her ghost.

"Grace?"

"Coming." Shoving aside her insecurities, she

hurried down the stairs, the frames on the treads rattling with every step.

"Something wrong?"

She shook her head and urged Lexi out of the cabin, helping the little girl into the extended cab of the truck and placing the framed portrait in the back with her. She turned only to find Seth behind her.

"I—I forgot to help you down the step. Sorry."

"No problem." His gaze probed hers. "What's wrong? You're shaking."

She swallowed the lump in her throat, fully conscious of the fact she couldn't battle Arie's memory, much less Earl's. How could she have been so stupid as to think she could? "It's nothing. Let's go."

Back at the house she followed Seth up the ramp and onto the porch, carrying Lexi in her arms. She made her way around the kitchen table and through to the family room when she stopped in her tracks.

"Merry Christmas," Brent said, grinning.

CHAPTER FOURTEEN

JAKE SNAGGED LEXI FROM her arms. "We've been waiting for you. Come on, Lex. See you all in the morning. Brent, bud, we'll catch up tomorrow."

"Sure thing," Brent answered, still grinning at her. He held his arms open. "Well? Aren't you going to say anything? I thought you'd be pleased to see me."

"What? Oh, I am!" She flew across the room and wrapped her arms around her little brother, laughing as he picked her up off her feet. "I am!" she repeated, hugging him before he put her down. She took in his bright green eyes and mischievous grin. "I'm also surprised! How'd you get here? When?"

Brent laughed. "A plane, a little while ago, and you can thank Seth," he added. "I sold one of my inventions and called because I wanted to see you, and Seth invited me to stay."

Grace didn't know what to say. To do. So she did the only thing she could. She untangled herself from Brent, retraced her steps across the floor and bent to kiss Seth on the cheek. "Thank you," she whispered, eyes open on his as her mouth grazed his stubbled jaw. A shiver raced through her at the contact. "I…we haven't spent Christmas together in *years.*"

"I know." Seth smiled as she drew back, and he thumbed a tendril of hair away from her cheek, slid his palm around her neck and brought her the couple of inches it took to press his mouth briefly to hers in a kiss full of want and need and—

"Want me to leave you two alone?"

Sputtering, Grace pulled away and glanced down at Seth in embarrassment, only to find a broad smile covering his face. "Just getting my good-night kiss. Brent, nice to see you again. Jake and Maura get you settled in all right?"

"Yeah, it's great. Thanks a lot for letting me stay."

"No problem. Let us know if you need anything. I'll let you catch up with Grace and see you in the morning." Seth squeezed the fingers of her hand and brought them to his lips for a kiss. "Good-night, Grace. Thanks for the date. I'll, uh, see you later."

Seth spun himself around and headed down the hall. Awkward silence filled the room until Seth's bedroom door closed. Grace turned to face her brother.

Brent waited a moment, then asked, "You two are dating again?"

"N-Not exactly—"

"You're blushing."

"It's warm in here."

She got a cheeky grin in response. "Come on. Give it up. You came here to help him, you went out on a date with him, you kissed him. That's dating."

Her mouth trembled despite her attempt to control her emotions. "Oh, Brent." She dropped down onto the nearby couch and buried her face in her hands with a moan. "I'm so confused."

Brent sat on the couch beside her. "Talk to me."

"Where do I begin?" She leaned against him and shook her head. "Brent, he's a *patient*."

"Who also used to be your boyfriend."

She pulled away far enough to see his face. "We didn't date long before we left North Star—"

"Long enough. Besides, you've told me you're getting tired of the traveling all over the country. Sounds to me like you're in the mood to settle down somewhere and fall in love."

"I never said anything about falling in love."

That got a laugh out of him. "You don't have to," he said as he squeezed her. "It's written all over your face when you look at him. Deny it all you want, but you've always loved him, Grace. Any idiot could see that."

"You're wrong."

"Yeah? Maybe. I guess it would be tough with him in a chair now and all."

Her jaw dropped and she yanked away. "*That has nothing to do with it!* Brent, how dare you say something like that."

He shrugged. "Hey, it's a legitimate statement. After caring for patients all these years, you have to admit it would be tough to come home to it to boot."

Her temper deflated at his honesty. "It's not that."

"Then what's bothering you?"

It took her a moment to find the words. "Can I ask you something?"

"What are brothers for?"

She stared into the flames. "Does it bother you, what Earl said? I mean, do you constantly have him in your head telling you how worthless and lazy and pathetic—"

"Yeah," Brent said quietly. "He's there. How can he not be since he destroyed our childhood? But I tagged along with you to enough counseling sessions to know we can't let him destroy our whole lives, Grace. Is that what's bothering you about Seth?"

She hesitated, then shrugged. "Maybe… Some," she admitted slowly. "I know it's wrong and stupid and childish, but how can I possibly compare to his wife?"

"You can't," Brent informed her bluntly. "And you shouldn't be trying to."

"I know, but…"

Brent took her hand in his. "I'm sorry for asking you to stay, Grace. After Earl found out you weren't his, you took Mom's place as his punching bag and—"

"He hit you, too," she murmured. "And where would we have gone? At fourteen and ten, our options were limited. If anyone's to blame, it's Earl. I know that, but believing it sometimes is hard."

"Why?"

She lifted her shoulder in a shrug. "You've never wondered if you weren't good enough? If maybe that's why he…he hit us and stuff? Never wondered if we'd only been better Mom would've come back?"

Brent looked away, and in that moment, Grace wished she'd never spoken her thoughts aloud.

"Yeah, I have. But what are we supposed to do, Grace? Stop living? I want things out of life, good things. A home, family. If I let them take that away from me, I'm letting two people who didn't deserve to be parents take away my chance."

Brent stared at her, his gaze direct and searching. "Consider dating Seth as your chance to put the past to rest and move on," he said. "Seth's a nice guy and you've known Jake a long time, so you've got a solid basis for comparison. They're nothing like Earl."

"I know that."

"Then why not go for it? Let Seth help you get Earl out of your head once and for all."

A CRY PIERCED THE NIGHT, frightened and full of pain. Seth sat up, grabbed his chair and swung into it. Grace cried out a second time before he got himself situated and the door open to wheel himself through. She hadn't had a nightmare in a while and he'd begun to hope their midnight talks were helping her heal.

"No. No, don't!" she whimpered.

"Grace?" Seth raced to her as fast as he could, but she was in the middle of the large bed and he couldn't reach her. He transferred out of the wheelchair and onto the mattress beside her, hating that it took him so long. "Grace, honey, wake up."

She flung her arm, fist closed, toward him. *"Don't!"*

Seth grabbed hold of her hand. "You're dreaming, sweetheart. It's all right, it's just a dream." He propped himself up with an elbow, one hand clasping hers, the other brushing her damp, tangled hair off her face. Her skin was soft, silky smooth, but wet with tears and sweat.

His breath lodged in his lungs. Earl Korbit was dead, but he wished him dead a hundred times over. A thousand. How could a man rape a woman? A *child.*

Grace jerked upright with a startled shriek. She yanked on the hand he held and glared at him with furious, sleep-glazed eyes. "No!"

"Sweetheart, it's okay. It's me, Seth. It was a dream. Just a dream, that's all."

Slowly her confusion cleared and she crumpled. "Seth?"

He reached out and gently tucked her hair behind her ear before wiping away the first in a stream of tears. She'd left the light on in her bathroom, the door mostly closed, and in the muted light he could see how badly she trembled. Unable to do anything more, he opened his arms.

Grace dove into his embrace and he smoothed his hand over her, the tense muscles of her back, her shoulders, neck. Held her close. Sweet, amazing Grace. His saving grace.

Minutes ticked by, the silence broken by her sobs and ragged breathing slowly returning to normal. After a long, long while she raised her head. Seth stroked her cheek with his thumb, saw her gaze lower to his mouth. He didn't move, didn't blink. Barely breathed as Grace leaned toward him and pressed her mouth to his. Her eyes were open, searching, as her tongue touched his. Then she lowered her lashes and deepened the kiss, her desperation to forget the past lending a frantic edge.

He understood the need to forget. The desire to

lose himself in something or someone. Whatever it took to make the pain go away.

Grace whimpered, the tiny sound caught between their mouths. Her hands ran over his bare chest, lingered on the muscles of his arms and squeezed as though she liked the feel of him. She tore her mouth from his and stared at him, and in that moment something shifted. A wall fell right before his eyes.

"This is—you can't—can't be comfortable," she said shyly, biting her lip as she shifted on the bed to give him more room.

"Help me with my legs," he urged, for once not minding that she did indeed have to help him. When he lay on her bed with his back against the pillowed headboard, her eyes widened ever so slightly when she saw his erection tenting the material of his flannel pants.

"Whatever you want to do, honey. We'll only go as far as you allow," he promised, even as he prayed for strength. He wanted her now. Right now. But he'd find a way to hold himself back. "I'll hold you all night long if you want. Nothing else. You call the shots."

He swallowed as tears filled her eyes once more. Gritted his teeth when she fought so hard to hold them back. She'd been brutalized and hurt and now that someone offered her tenderness and love, she didn't know what to make of it. Didn't know how to react.

"I want m-more," she whispered. "But I don't—I don't know what will happen later. You know, when…"

"Neither do I," he murmured, reaching out to stroke her cheek. "But maybe together we can figure it out as it happens."

She wet her lips, sniffling, attempting to smile. "Okay."

Okay. What a simple word. Grace wanted him as much as he wanted her, but there was an extreme possibility she'd panic and run. Just as there was an extreme possibility he couldn't maintain an erection long enough to get through the act.

He told himself that whatever happened, happened, that he'd trust in the man upstairs and let nature take its course. He opened his arms. "Come here."

Grace slid closer, one last remaining tear trickling down her cheek as she lowered herself to his side. Seth caught the tear with a fingertip and brought it to his mouth to taste, conscious that she watched him. But when he took her pain inside himself, he wasn't prepared for her reaction. She surged toward him and followed his finger with her lips.

She kissed him. Wild and heady, urgent. Grace kissed as if she was trying to outdistance her memories. Deep, passionate, sensual matings of lips and teeth and tongue.

She tore her mouth from his and worked her way lower, exploring his chest and shoulders, his stomach, gently biting the skin below his belly button.

He couldn't have stopped the growl that escaped his chest if his life depended on it because the sensation there was so powerful, maybe more so than before his accident.

"Grace. Ah, honey—"

Liking the sound of his husky, desire-filled voice, Grace bit lightly again, relishing his groan. She sat up on the bed next to him and, hands trembling, pulled her nightgown over her head, avoiding his gaze as she let the material drop to the floor.

She waited, wanting to memorize every moment. Every kiss and caress. Every look that told her Seth's words weren't platitudes, but true. Seth made her feel beautiful and bold, capable and carefree, and she wanted more than anything to make love with him.

As if reading her thoughts, Seth smiled a wickedly sensual smile that stole her breath. He lifted a work-roughened hand to her waist and ever so slowly smoothed his knuckles up her body to the curve of her breast, around and around the tip. She inhaled as deeply as her burning lungs would allow, the sensations buffeting her senses.

"You okay?"

Oh, yes. A sound escaped her, one that probably

should've mortified her seeing as how it was so revealing but—

"I'll take that as a yes. Let me taste you, sweetheart."

Her lashes were heavy, her body tingling and hot. She parted her lips in an attempt to draw in more air, but it didn't help. Seth wanted her closer— she wanted to be closer—but the way he sat leaning against the headboard meant she had to kneel on the bed beside him to be at the right height or else straddle his waist and—

His fingers pressed against the base of her spine above her panties and urged her up, up. Then he leaned forward until his mouth caught her breast. Grace shut her eyes with a moan as every tug of his lips sent a stab of hunger through to her very core.

He guided her leg over his stomach. Broad hands massaged her back, lower, and under the elastic of her panties to cup her bottom. She gasped, held her breath as Seth gently ground her against him. He suckled harder and suddenly the gentleness in his hands wasn't enough. She needed more. More pressure, more touching, more Seth. When the sensations became too much, Grace pulled away and moved backward until she eased the length of him beneath her. Just *there*.

The past reared itself, tried to intrude, but she determinedly shoved it away.

This was Seth. *Seth.*

He groaned and leaned his head back against the headboard. "Ah, honey, we've got to slow down or I'm going to—"

She shifted, caught him just the right way and trapped him between her thighs. In response Seth pulled her mouth to his and plunged his tongue inside. His hesitation, his overly protective gentleness was gone, and her body hummed with excitement. With love.

Grace whimpered at her thoughts, at the feel of Seth's hands insistently moving her up, off him, so he could remove her panties. Once again she faltered, fought her fear, but when she opened her eyes and locked her gaze on his, her confidence returned. As long as she could see him, know it was Seth, she wasn't afraid.

"You're so beautiful, Grace. Beautiful inside and out."

His voice rumbled out of his chest, rough and gravelly with need. Shivers racked her body as his hand stroked her leg, her thigh, and she moved, helped him have better access and moaned when he found her, wet and warm. Ready for him. Like in all the books she'd read, the ones where the man and woman loved each other and sex wasn't brutal.

"Protection. Ah, I don't—I can't believe this. I'm sorry, Grace. So sorry."

Her pulse pounded in her veins. "I'm safe." She paused. "I—I've been tested. More than once," she said even as her face heated in shame. Earl could've done a lot more damage than he had, but thankfully God had watched out for her. "I'm…I'm also on birth control. To regulate my cycles."

Seth's grin was filled with such relief she laughed softly. Imagine that. Laughter and sex. Fun.

With wicked intent he went back to nibbling the sensitive skin of her neck. "Me, too. Safe. Help me, Grace. My pants."

She lowered her hands to his pajama pants, grateful for the drawstring that allowed her easy access. Seth braced his hands on the bed and lifted himself up as she pulled the pants down. He wasn't wearing anything underneath.

As soon as the flannel was out of the way she crawled on top of him again, her body all too eager for more of the magic Seth had shown it. His hands were everywhere, soothing, lightly pinching, making her squirm and constrict and sigh so fiercely she wondered how he'd ever make it better. This was what it was like? How it was supposed to be?

She laughed softly, happy. Sad. Teary.

"You okay?"

She nodded, her throat too full to speak, eyes too full to see clearly. So she did the only other thing she knew to do. She nudged him with her body, unerringly placed the tip of him within her warmth and echoed his groan of pleasure. Hesitating, she tried to relax, and then lowered herself a bit more. Grace stared into Seth's eyes as she let herself sink down, down, until she held all of him.

"So beautiful. Ah, Grace." His hands gripped her hips and Seth began lifting and lowering her against him, slow at first, then urgently. She was ready for him, and so surprised there wasn't any pain. There'd always been pain.

She whimpered softly, the pleasure of Seth's body joined with hers too much to withstand. Tears gathered once again and she swallowed them back, fighting to maintain control.

"I can't. Too long. Not going to last—"

A sob broke free before she could stop it and she could feel Seth tense. Another sob had Seth groaning and desperately trying to still the movement of her hips, but she wouldn't let him. She grabbed his hands and didn't let go, pressing them to the bed so she could keep up the pace that would bring him release.

"Honey, stop. *Stop,* Grace, you're crying."

Her mouth covered his, and even though she couldn't stem the flowing tears she kept moving, up and down, grinding herself against Seth in a way that made him catch his breath. She wanted to please him as much as he'd pleased her by getting her through this moment. For sharing and showing her how powerful love could be.

Needing to feel him surround her, she pressed Seth's hands to her breasts, wanting him to touch her, hold her. "For you," she whispered hoarsely, her words more a sob than sounds.

Seth groaned and shifted forward, shoving himself off the headboard until he was able to wrap her in his arms. He cradled her against him while his mouth pressed kisses all over her face and neck.

The change of position shifted her, made his penetration deeper, and her desperate lunges of before were gone. In their place was a slow, rocking give-and-take. One that calmed the pace, slowed it to a bearable degree and then began to rebuild the passion her sobs had weakened.

Sniffling, she raised her gaze to his, loving the feel of him inside her. A gruff sound exploded from his chest as Seth climaxed, and at that pleasure-filled sight, her heart and soul broke free, free from the past. Free from guilt and responsibility.

"Mine," Seth breathed as he slipped his hand between them. "My beautiful Grace."

She started when he touched her. Automatically pulled away, but the arm he had wrapped around her waist slipped to her hips and he continued to grind her against him.

"It's okay, Seth. It was perfect."

"It will be," he corrected before he caught her mouth and kissed her.

A moan escaped as desire rocketed through her, forcing her to tear her mouth from his and bite her lips as the combined motion of his still-hard arousal inside her and his stroking fingers brought her to life again. She arched into his touch.

"That's it. This is for both of us, Grace. Come for me."

With a whimper that turned into a broken cry she tipped over the edge into bliss unlike anything she'd ever anticipated. She exploded, flew. Melted from the inside out and came crashing down. Her forehead dropped to his shoulder and she curled her limp arms around him as she tried to breathe, to cope.

Seth held her as he fell back against the headboard with her locked in his arms, pressing kiss after kiss to her forehead, her face. Her mouth.

How could it be? How could something that had been so ugly be so beautiful? Natural. Joyous and spiritual.

"I love you, Grace. I love you."

CHAPTER FIFTEEN

SETH AWOKE AND FOUND the bed empty. He looked at the clock on the nightstand: 2:00 a.m. He shifted and checked the room, but he already knew Grace wasn't there. After making love, after telling her he loved her, he'd fallen asleep like some loser instead of talking to her, pressing her for answers and insights to what they'd shared.

He sat up and grabbed the arm of his wheelchair to haul it close and make the transfer. The distant sound of a shower running made him hurry; bending over, he lifted his right foot onto the support, then his left.

He wheeled himself around until he reached the open door between their rooms. Grace was showering in his bathroom. And after everything they'd shared he knew he should probably give her privacy to come to terms with the latest development in their relationship, but he was terrified she'd had another nightmare. Could he have slept through it? Grace might have gotten up to keep from disturbing him. It was just the sort of thing she'd do.

He raced across the room and opened the bathroom door.

Grace was huddled on the floor of the glass-enclosed shower, crying. No, what she was doing couldn't be called crying. She sobbed so hard she gasped for breath, the little moans and noises escaping her lips muffled by the washcloth she held over her mouth. He stared at her, angry, *furious* that she sat there alone instead of coming to him and letting him help. When would she get it? Would she always have that struggle? That need to stand on her own and be independent instead of leaning on him?

Rolling closer, he opened the shower door and her head jerked up. Through the water beating down on her, through the hair hanging over her face, she stared at him. Her eyes red-rimmed and swollen. Haunted.

His anger fizzled. In her face he saw the child she'd been. The young girl who'd been used and abused by a man she should've been able to trust. Rage threatened to overwhelm him, but he swallowed it back, determined he'd maintain control of himself for Grace's sake. Without comment, he transferred out of his chair and onto the built-in bench. She stiffened but didn't move, stayed huddled in a ball on the shower floor.

Seth lowered his hand to her wet hair and gently rubbed, smoothing his hand over the sopping length and hoping, praying, for her to let him inside her protective walls. Finally, as though she couldn't bear the weight any longer, she lowered her head until her cheek rested against his leg. Then they sat there in silence, his hand moving slowly over her bent head, the water raining down on them both.

Long moments passed with nothing but the shower filling the silence. Grace wiped her face with the cloth in her hands and relished the sense of safety surrounding her. Making love with him had been unbelievably beautiful and powerful and *special*. And it had made her furious. So angry she wanted to scream and shout at the injustice.

Earl had taken something intimate and exquisite and turned it into a nightmare. Degrading, torturous, a punishment and humiliation she never should've had to endure. But with Seth—oh, she'd found herself again. Found a part of herself she'd very nearly convinced herself Earl had destroyed.

Seth's broad hand slid down her hair and he murmured a soothing sound over the rush of water. She didn't respond, couldn't. So she merely held on to him in an undignified heap and wished things were different. All she wanted to do was curl up in Seth's lap and relive the magic and love she'd found in his arms. Experience it, cherish it, hold it within her heart forever.

Following her thoughts, she pressed a kiss to his

calf, his knee. His thigh. Tiny little kisses, chaste, but his reaction was instantaneous, matching the answering one deep in her body that stirred to life and warmed her from the inside out.

"Grace—" His hands shifted to cradle her face, his thumbs smoothing over her chin and lips. His eyes so full of tenderness and desire and—

She shut her mind off to what he'd said and let him urge her to her knees, to her feet, arrange her until she straddled his lap. His mouth devoured hers, and even as her eyes burned from her crying spell, her body burned for his touch. Ached for the blaze of his hands as they roamed her body and teased it into welcoming him inside her.

This time their passion was slow and steady, sensual in its simplicity. Infinitely powerful and sweet and...*loving*.

She whimpered softly, their mouths melding together in a long, voracious kiss. She rocked against him, lost to her thoughts, to the feel of him as Seth gripped the bench with one hand to keep them both balanced. With the other he stroked her body, up to her breast to squeeze and gently pinch, down, between her legs to rub where they joined, over and over until she couldn't breathe properly. Her pace increased and his body slid into hers with more and more force. Force she controlled.

Her climax slammed into her, catching her off

guard, and her moans filled her ears, echoing off the shower enclosure. She smiled when he groaned out his release, laughed softly as she bucked against him and he completely lost control and they nearly fell off the seat.

She wrapped her arms around his neck, her knees folded up at his sides, and listened as his ragged breath panted into her ear.

"Grace, ah, Grace, I love you. Marry me."

Pain knifed through her. She shoved his hand away and jerked to her feet before turning to face the spray.

Marry him?

What did you think would happen?

She knew Seth's sense of honor. His pride. Knew he didn't take things lightly, and the fact that he knew about her past and still made love to her would undoubtedly make him feel…guilty. Responsible. Seth was such an honorable man. One of the last of a dying breed of men. A fact proved by the way he'd married Arie after discovering she was pregnant. Now after making love to her, knowing her secret, he believed he owed her more as well. Believed he had to care for her, protect her from her past even though her many hang ups could potentially destroy them as a couple.

"No."

"No?"

"You don't want to marry me."

He caressed her hip. "Yes, I do," he corrected, his voice firm.

"Then I'm sorry, because I *can't.*"

"Why? No, come on, Grace, talk to me."

She flicked a hand toward the rapidly cooling spray. "We've got to get out of here."

Seth twisted the water off. "Fine. But you're not running away from me. We're going to talk about this. About *us.*"

Grace stepped from the shower and wrapped a towel around herself, all too conscious of his gaze on her. And all too conscious of her response. She was so tempted. She wanted to be with him. Wanted to marry him.

But she couldn't.

"That was a mistake."

"Bull." Seth took the towel she tossed at him and began to roughly dry himself off. "It was perfect. It was exactly what was supposed to happen between us."

Her disbelieving burst of laughter earned her a glare. "I'll get you some clothes."

"I want to marry you, Grace. I want to spend my life with you, and I think you feel the same way, but you're too afraid to believe me. You're letting your past interfere with your future. It's almost like you're too afraid to let it go because it's the only thing you've known." Seth got into his wheelchair and she watched the ease of his movements, thankful he'd draped the towel over his waist.

"Seth…there will come a time when you're better and then you might not feel the same way about me."

"I *love* you."

"Because I've helped you!" She couldn't meet his gaze. "I'm sorry about what just happened—"

"You're a horrible liar, Grace. You're scared. Maybe the first time we made love took you by surprise since you'd woken up from the nightmare, but what happened in that shower wasn't a mistake, honey. You were wide awake, and there's no denying you wanted me just as much as I wanted you."

She shoved a hand through her dripping hair, unable to acknowledge he was right. Too frightened to admit she wasn't strong enough to let go of the barriers she'd erected through the years to protect her from being hurt again. "Y-Yes, but—"

He inched closer. "But what? What are you so afraid of? That I won't recover? Or that I will? I'm *not* Earl! I'd never use my strength against you. I'm not some pervert who likes to hurt little girls."

She shook her head, the movement slinging water off her hair. "I *can't*." She ran a shaking hand over her face. "You're right, I woke up after the nightmare and you were there and— Thank you…for helping me but—"

"You're thanking me?"

She nodded rapidly and tried to ignore the look of pain her words caused him. "For showing me that sex—"

"We made love, Grace. We didn't have sex and I want you to *marry* me! Now, let's sit down like two adults and talk about this."

"Grace?" Jake's panicked voice came from within Grace's bedroom.

Grace blanched, but before she could move Jake saw them through the open doorway, his eyes wild with fear. His gaze swept over them, but Jake didn't comment on their state of undress or their obvious change in relationship.

"Maura's in labor," he said as he yanked on his coat.

"Have you called a squad?"

Jake shook his head. "I can't get through. It's snowing, icy. Freak storm blew in. I'm going to go get the chains on the truck and drive her."

"I'll go check on Maura," Grace murmured as she clutched the towel around her body and pushed past Jake.

Seth wheeled himself closer. "How are you going to drive her in your condition? I'll keep calling the squad. Maybe they can meet you."

Jake nodded, nostrils flaring with every breath, his hands trembling so badly he couldn't fasten his coat. Seth hated his helplessness in the sight of Jake's torment so he went to the phone and dialed for help. The line was busy.

"I'll keep calling. Everything will be fine."

Jake wiped a hand over his sweaty face, then lunged out of the room. "I hope so. It's too early for the baby. She's got more than three weeks to go."

Seth nodded and punched in the number again.

HALF AN HOUR LATER Grace brushed sweat-matted hair off Maura's forehead and forced herself to smile. Jake's wife was curled up on the bed, the blankets under her soaked from where her water had broken. One way or another, the baby was coming.

"You're doing great. Try to relax. I'm going to take your blood pressure again, okay? Just relax."

Maura moaned. "This isn't exactly what I had in mind for a delivery."

"I know," she soothed. "But everything's going to be fine. You've got to take me shopping, remember? Now that Brent's ready to graduate I need help picking out a dress to wear unless I'm going to show up in sweats or my one and only black dress."

Maura smiled. "Should've let me cut a few feet off the hem so Seth could see those long legs of yours. Too bad my clothes didn't fit." She shifted uncomfortably.

"Hang in there," Grace soothed. "Jake's outside. He's signaling for the helicopter. Good thing he has friends in high places, because you're going to get a ride."

Maura's attempt to smile failed. "Always too afraid to fly," she muttered, her breath rasping in and out of her chest. "Figures that my first trip would be in a snowstorm."

Grace laughed softly, pleased with Maura's attempt to combat her fright with humor. "You're going to be fine. You'll make it to the hospital, deliver there and be home in no time."

Grace looked over her shoulder to the empty doorway as another contraction racked Maura's frame. She glanced at her watch to time it.

"I've never...seen anything like it," Maura groaned softly. "Seth looks at you and..." Her breath wheezed out of her lungs as she panted through the pain. "Lights up."

"Jake's the same way with you."

"They're good men."

Grace heard the approaching *thump-thump-thump* of a helicopter's blades. "They're here." And she was relieved. "It won't be long now."

"You slept...with Seth." Maura frowned at her. "Jake couldn't find you so I told him to check Seth's room."

Knowing she couldn't hide anything from her new

friend, Grace sighed. "It—It shouldn't have happened."

Maura shifted against the pillow behind her. "He loves you."

Jake rushed into the bedroom, his dark hair and coat layered with snow. Downstairs, Seth's voice rose as he spoke to someone and then there were more footsteps on the stairs. Paramedics rushed into the room with a gurney. Grace stood to get out of the way, but Maura's hand caught hers.

"No matter what happened in your past, Grace, life is too short to deny love. And please, don't hurt Seth again."

Tears burned her eyes as she bent and kissed Maura, conscious that someone's hands pulled at her to try to hurry her away. "It'll be all right. Don't worry. You just go have this baby so I can hold him or her before I leave Montana."

JUST AFTER DAWN Seth gave up on getting any sleep and settled himself in his wheelchair. He lifted his right foot onto the support, then his left. The metal was cold and goose bumps shot up his legs.

Cold?

He felt the metal support. It wasn't his imagination, wasn't him wanting to recover so badly he'd only imagined the sensations.

He swung himself around and hurriedly wheeled

himself to the gym, anxious to see if he had the guts to put his feet where his mind traveled.

His heart pounded, thumping with excitement and dread as he positioned himself in front of the parallel bars and locked the wheels. He bent and used his hands to raise and lower his feet to the padded floor after adjusting the supports out of his way. Jake and his family needed him. His ranch needed him. And Grace needed a man able to help her conquer her fears.

He sent up a silent prayer as he gripped the bars. His hands were damp, but he pulled himself to his feet and quickly locked his arms to hold his position. He struggled to stand fully erect, and after a moment sweat dripped into his eyes and stung. But a little sting was nothing compared to what was happening in his leg. He *burned.*

His sweaty hand slipped on the bar and he wobbled slightly before he caught himself. Fire clawed at him, the sensation near his foot changing from burning and stinging to pure, unadulterated pain. He gasped as the hurt spread like a wild fire. Up his calf, his knee. Oh, God help him, his thigh and even parts of his groin. He dropped his head forward and growled.

"Seth?" Grace's tone was soft, not meant to startle, and now that he knew she was there, she hurried around the bars to stand in front of him, the smile on her face nothing short of breathtaking. "Seth, you're doing wonderfully! Concentrate. Slow, deep breaths. Hold the pose for as long as possible."

He did as she instructed, breathed deeply in order to combat the pain, but just staring at her created a different type of pain. A different kind of need. What would he do if she left him again?

"Uncle Seff!"

Had it not been for Lexi's voice he wouldn't have known what hit him. One minute he struggled to remain standing as he stared into Grace's beautiful face and the next, the gym tilted at an odd angle and Grace's expression turned to one of horror.

Grace reached for him, but it was too late. The force of Lexi barreling into him from behind had him going down on top of Grace in a tangle of arms and legs and grunts. Pain streaked through him and nausea followed, hitting him hard and fast. Through it all he was conscious of Grace beneath him, gasping for air from having a hundred-eighty-pound man drop on top of her with a forty-pound child squirming all over his burning legs.

He *felt* Lexi on his legs. Experienced every aspect of the unbearable pain she caused when she trampled him in an attempt to get up. "Lexi, get off! Oh, God." Seth lowered his head to Grace's chest. "Grace, help me. It *hurts.*"

GRACE WAS STILL SEEING STARS. She closed her eyes as her head spun. A distant part of her mind registered Lexi clambering on top of them and running from the room, but Seth's groans of pain were of more concern to her than his niece. He could *feel?*

She brushed her hands over his head, his back, feeling his sweat-drenched T-shirt and trembling body.

"Grace. Sorry. Oh, God, help me, it hurts so bad."

The sound of his pain put her in motion. She wormed out from beneath him, careful not to jar Seth any more than necessary. "You *feel?*"

His breathing ragged, his mouth was bracketed by white lines of pain in a face nearly purple with strain. "Yes. Ah, yes. Hot coals burning me alive."

"Since when? When you stood or—"

"Before," he muttered. "Tingles and heat. Some cold. I thought I'd imagined it all."

Grace frowned, angry and hurt he'd kept something so important from her. "Don't move. I'll call your doctor and see how quickly we can get you to the hospital for an MRI. We'll need a back brace and an ambulance—"

Seth shook his head and caught her hand in his, held her in position hunched over him. "No. Can't go anywhere in this weather."

"What the— Who won?" Brent asked from the doorway.

"Seth was standing at the parallel bars and Lexi knocked him down in her excitement," she explained quickly as she checked Seth for further injury.

"Youch." Brent's stride ate up the distance and he kneeled on the other side of Seth. "Can I help?"

"Where's Lexi?" she asked.

The words had no sooner left her mouth than the front door slammed shut and Grace looked up in horror.

There was a blizzard outside and Lexi had just taken off.

CHAPTER SIXTEEN

"GRACE, SHE CAN'T HAVE GONE far. Look in the barn
if she's not on the porch. Brent, help me back in my
chair."

Grace ran down the hall, grabbed her coat from
the peg and shrugged it on as she stepped outside,
thankful the wind hadn't obliterated the tiny footsteps visible in the snow.

"We'll follow you," Seth suddenly called from
behind her.

She turned and glared at Brent for pushing Seth
outside, taking in Seth's clothes, wet with sweat, his
face drained. "No, you won't. I can't concentrate on
Lexi if I'm worried about you. Go back inside and
watch to make sure she doesn't come out when I'm
not around to see her."

"Grace—"

"Brent, make sure he doesn't go anywhere!" She
waited for Brent's nod before leaving the porch and
hurrying across the wide yard to the barn. The wind
was strong, the snow blowing so sharply each flake

cut into the skin of her face. She pulled on the handle of the barn doors, but they wouldn't budge so she walked around to the paddock, holding on to the weathered wood for support when the wind nearly blew her off her feet. Climbing over the slippery metal rails without losing her balance took some doing, but she entered the barn through the entrance in the side.

Grace found herself surrounded by horses huddled together for warmth. They nickered when they saw her, shifting together with loud *thumps* of their hooves.

"Easy," she murmured, carefully keeping an eye on the horses until she could get out of the pen.

"I said come down!"

"No! Go away!"

Grace looked up, her eyes widening when she saw Lexi straddling a rafter over the barn's open middle, her chubby legs dangling thirty feet above-ground.

"I'll take the doll back if you don't come here," Roy threatened from his position in the loft, his words slurred.

"Uh-uh, you can't—she's mine."

Grace kept her mouth closed, not wanting to startle Lexi into falling. She crossed the floor to the ladder leading to the loft just as Roy reached out a hand and tried to snag one of Lexi's feet. A handful of hay fell to the ground floor, knocked off by his boot.

"You want me to tell your daddy you're up here? He's told you over and over to stay down." He reached for her again.

"No—"

Roy managed to grab Lexi's boot with one hand. "Get down *now!*" he ordered, pulling on her leg.

Grace raced up the ladder, hoping to calm the situation before Roy wound up yanking Lexi down off the rafter and hurting her. When she reached the loft she tripped over a nearly empty bottle of bourbon…and a porn magazine that had been tossed aside.

"Lexi, *don't move,*" she urged hoarsely.

The child stuck her lower lip out. "You're mad at me."

Grace forced a smile. "No, honey, I'm not. I know you didn't mean to knock your uncle Seth down. He's fine, okay? He's waiting for you, so why don't you come down and talk to him?" She slid a glance toward Roy and found him glaring at her, his hand still holding on to Lexi's foot. "Let go of her."

Lexi jerked her boot away and Roy reached out to grab her foot again, stumbled, then used the barn wall to steady himself. "You little—"

"Don't do that! She'll fall." Grace couldn't help

but cringe when Roy turned his full attention to her and gave her a salacious look. A lump of disgust clogged her throat and a shudder ran through her before she could stop it. "Get away from her and let her get down."

Roy leaned back against the barn wall directly under Lexi and raised a brow. "Why should I?" A grin spread over his features. "What'll I get in return?" he slurred. "You ready for a real man now?"

A trickle of sweat ran down her back despite seeing her breath in the frigid air. A real man? Seth was a real man. Caring and strong and oh so gentle. Not a drunken, perverted monster who liked to threaten women and children.

Maura's words took on new meaning. Life *was* too short. She wasn't the frightened little girl Earl had raped in the dark.

"Get away from her."

"It'll cost you." Roy's smile widened. "I want a kiss."

Which he'd use to force more. "Let her get down."

Roy took her comment as acceptance, his gaze sweeping from her face to her breasts and back again, the bulge in his pants obvious to someone who knew what it was.

"You want it bad, don't you?"

"Want what? Grace, if you stay, I wanna stay," Lexi grumbled, oblivious to the danger.

"Climb down and go to the house, Lexi. *Now,*" she ordered, her tone one the child immediately heeded.

Seth had called his niece a monkey and, sure enough, Lexi expertly maneuvered the rafters, scooting along the beam until she reached a point over the loft where two crates were stacked up.

Grace stepped forward to help, but Bernard grabbed Lexi by the waist and held on to her, walking the distance across the loft, past Grace, to set Lexi on her feet by the ladder.

"Can't I stay? Uncle Seff's prob'ly still mad at me."

"*Go,* Lexi."

Frowning, Lexi grabbed hold of the ladder and descended, her footsteps loud as she ran across the packed earthen floor.

"Well now…"

"I'm not going to kiss you."

Roy gave her a once-over and licked his lips. "Like hell."

Hands shaking, Grace shook her head. "Stay away from me."

"I let her go. What's the problem?"

"I said no."

"You screwed your own father, an' you're sayin' no to me?"

"Earl *raped* me and he wasn't my father!"

Bernard shrugged. "You were old enough."

She wanted to close her eyes, to retreat into that place she'd go when Earl abused her, but she couldn't. She wasn't a victim anymore, and she also wasn't entirely sure Lexi was gone.

Focus. Breathe deeply. She fought the darkness within her that almost overwhelmed her.

Roy stepped forward. "You're gonna like me, Grace. We'll get along fine while this storm blows through." He lunged at her then, closing the distance between them and grabbing her by the arm before she remembered her self-defense classes or could get away. Grace brought her knee up to emasculate him, but she hit his upper thigh instead.

Bernard cursed and used his greater weight to shove her down onto the wood planks. Pain sliced through her ribs. The dust and dirt layering the loft choked her. She couldn't breathe. Roy climbed on top of her, his hands yanking at her comfortable work-out pants, breaking the string and pulling them down even as his knees pried her legs apart. She twisted, her hands and nails clawing at him anywhere she could reach.

"Bitch!" He hit her hard. Knocked her head back until her skull struck the loft's floor. Bright pinpoints of light appeared before her eyes, and desperate, she twisted, frantic, the move allowing her to roll completely over onto her back. She reached out blindly and raked her nails down his face.

Roy cursed, grabbed her hands, and Grace used the change of position to bring her knee up again. This time her aim was true and she nailed him in the groin as hard as she could, relishing his growl of pain.

Still, he didn't let go. No, his grip squeezed until her fingers tingled and went numb, then he shifted both her hands into one of his as he straddled her waist and backhanded her.

"You like it rough? Well, baby, I can get as rough as you want."

Gracie-baby, you're just like her. Your mama liked it like this.

Grace shoved Earl's voice aside and deliberately went limp, closed her eyes and prayed her trick would work and Roy would think she'd fainted. It was nearly impossible to stay still, but she was rewarded when he paused, his breathing ragged and loud, the smell of alcohol nearly making her gag.

Roy straightened and released a grunt of satisfaction, a low, harsh laugh, and then shifted to one side. He yanked at her pants, one-handed, but when he was able to pull them down without her protest, he freed her hands with a jubilant laugh.

That's when she moved. Grace didn't hesitate. She hit Roy Bernard for all she was worth and scrambled out from under him, but the floor was slippery with loose hay and she couldn't get to her feet fast enough. Roy downed her again, cursing and laughing at the same time as he ground himself against her buttocks. Grace reached out and clawed for the edge of the loft, desperate to escape, when her fingers found the handle of a pitchfork. She gripped it tight as she tossed herself over onto her back and swung with all her might.

Everything happened in slow motion.

Roy's eyes widened and he lunged to the side to avoid the tines of the pitchfork, but in their battle they'd gotten closer to the edge. And when he scrambled out of the way, he kept going—going— all the way over to the barn floor below.

Abrupt silence filled the air and Grace hesitated, too shocked to do more than stare at the spot where Roy had disappeared. Dazed, in pain, she peered over the edge, spying Roy's body lying motionless on the floor, his head bleeding.

She clamped a hand over her mouth and moaned at the sight, at the pain in her side, her back. Her face. Wondered if her ribs were broken or simply bruised. The ladder was right there, but the effort it would take to climb down seemed insurmountable.

Surely Brent would come find her soon.

Stars danced before her eyes and she lowered her head to her arm just as a gun blast splintered the air.

SETH COULDN'T BELIEVE HIS EYES.

He'd waited for Grace and Lexi on the porch, but

not long after she'd gone around to the side and entered the barn, one of Jake's deputy friends had slowly driven his SUV up the snow-covered driveway to check on them. The deputy had taken one look at his pain-ridden face, waited while Brent explained what had happened, and was in the process of asking if Seth needed a ride to the hospital himself when Lexi crawled out from under the lowest fence rails, sobbing her heart out.

Brent ran over and snatched Lexi up, carrying her back to Seth and setting her in his lap. A quick check proved she was physically unharmed, but it took a while to get her calmed down enough to understand she was angry because Grace had ordered her to go to the house so she could kiss Roy.

About that time the wind died down, and Seth and Brent stared at each other in shock when they heard Grace scream. The deputy and Brent took off at a run, and Seth ordered Lexi into the house, desperate to get to Grace.

The barn doors were fastened shut from the inside, so while Brent went around through the side, the deputy blasted through the front.

Seth struggled to wheel himself through the snow, praying the whole time. Lagging way behind the others, he finally made it to the barn and saw the deputy kneeling beside Roy.

"He's unconscious."

"Where's Grace?" Seth asked, his gaze searching for her.

Brent ran toward them from the rear, looking in the tack room, the stalls. Seth wheeled himself deeper into the barn, his fear nearly drowning him.

"Grace!"

"Up…up here."

He looked up to see her hand hanging over the side of the loft and cursed his inability to get to her. Brent climbed the ladder and long, torturous seconds passed as he heard Brent asking her questions, murmuring reassurances.

"Is she all right? Brent, what's going on?"

"I'm okay," Grace called, her tone filled with pain.

The deputy climbed the ladder and helped Brent get Grace to the edge of the loft, her coat draped over her shoulders. She had one arm wrapped around her side and her breathing was ragged and shallow. Her hair was loose and full of straw. The sight of her bloodied mouth, the stiff way she moved, terrified him.

The deputy moved slowly down the ladder so he could assist Grace in turning and maneuvering without falling, but once on solid ground Grace's legs gave way despite the deputy's hold and she sank to the barn floor. Her coat slid off her shoulders and Brent draped it around her again, tucking it close for warmth. The deputy shot him a guarded look and that's when Seth noticed her workout pants weren't tied, realized her shirt was ripped and hanging open, her bra visible beneath.

Seth wheeled close and smoothed his hand over her bowed head, and Grace automatically turned toward him, leaned against his legs much like she had in the shower just hours ago. He bent forward and wrapped her in his arms, his eyes burning.

"Lexi?" she cried suddenly, jerking away from him and dazedly searching the barn.

"Shh. She's in the house. She's fine, safe."

"I'll go check on her," Brent volunteered, his gaze bright with worry.

Seth had to clear his throat twice. "What happened?"

She blinked. "When I got in—inside the barn she was up in the rafters. Roy said—he said if I wanted to get her down I had to k-kiss him."

Seth noticed the deputy pull a notepad from his belt and begin taking notes. He motioned with his hand for Seth to keep Grace talking.

"What happened then?" he urged.

Grace trembled and shook as she told them Bernard wouldn't take no for an answer. How he'd ripped her pants, pawed her, tried to rape her.

Seth couldn't stand it any longer. He shoved the

locks of his chair into place and bent, carefully lifting Grace onto his lap. Sobbing, she curled against him and cried.

TWO DAYS LATER GRACE finally managed to escape the house and Seth and Brent's overprotective smothering. At first she simply wanted to get away from the chaos since neighbors and friends had been bombarding the ranch seeking news, gossip and a peek at Jake and Maura's two newest additions to the family.

Grace smiled slightly and shoved her hair out of her face, wincing when the move strained her ribs. Since she couldn't head out the door for a run as she liked to do when she had something on her mind, she'd discreetly borrowed the keys to Jake's truck and disappeared.

But now she'd surprised herself by driving to Earl's grave.

It wasn't a conscious decision on her part to go there. In fact, when she stopped the truck outside the picket-fenced cemetery and stared at the marker atop his grave, the only thing she wanted to do was turn around and never look back.

But she didn't.

Figuring it was too late to be a coward now, she opened the door and faced the cold, gingerly exiting the vehicle and feeling every ache and pain in her body from her fight with Roy. Traversing the distance to the plain grave was harder, every step taking her closer and deeper into the past.

Earl Carlton Korbit. Not beloved father or husband. Simply her stepfather's name, date of birth and death. As she stared at the marker, it became harder to breathe, harder still to concentrate as she relived every slap and curse, every violation of her little-girl body.

"Oh, God, help me," she prayed, closing her eyes and lifting her face toward the sky, arms wrapped around herself against the cold, bitter air and the pain.

Seth, Brent—both of them said to let the past go, and she wanted to. She desperately wanted to. But how?

The Lord's Prayer came to her then, every word seemingly sent from heaven directly to her mind.

As we forgive those who trespass against us.

Tears threatened and she blinked rapidly, shaking her head. No, she couldn't. Earl wasn't worth forgiveness.

But if she couldn't forgive him, how could she ever truly put the past behind her?

There was a bench by the gate, and after knocking off a half foot of snow, she sat staring blankly at the rows of stone. Maybe she couldn't forgive Earl, but maybe she could find the strength to gain acceptance.

She nodded once. Acceptance. The past had happened and no amount of wishing or dreaming or praying was going to alter it. So maybe the key to moving on was being able to simply accept that her rape had happened. No excuses, no guilt. It happened and she had to deal with it. Use what she knew from personal experience to help others as a way of contending with it herself. Maybe acceptance would lead to forgiveness over time.

As if sensing her decision, the wind picked up, blowing her hair into her face. She swept it back with a bruised hand, her gaze once again drawn to the stone marker five yards away.

Grace leaned her head back and stared up at the cloudy, dark purple sky, the resolve she sought settling in her heart, her soul. She was a firm believer that things happened for a reason, and if that were the case, her rape had also happened for a reason.

To make her stronger? To lead her in a new direction? A shiver coursed through her, so powerful she knew she'd found her answer.

If that were the case, if what had happened to her was to prepare her to save other little girls, children, then it was worth it.

If that were the case, she could accept what happened…and move on with her life.

CHAPTER SEVENTEEN

AN HOUR LATER GRACE EASED herself back in the recliner Hank had kindly brought to her room after being treated and released from the hospital. Lying down was in no way comfortable or possible with her broken ribs, so she'd spent the last two nights sleeping in the chair, upright, Seth in her bed since he refused to leave her side in case she needed something during the night.

She closed her eyes, totally drained from her drive and the emotional release, but managed to smile when she heard an infant's cry from somewhere in the house. Pretty soon the single cry became a double and both baby boys were wailing loudly. Jake's sons bellowed like pros despite being premature.

She shifted uncomfortably, the pain medication she'd taken upon arriving home sliding into her blood and finally beginning to take effect, easing the tension coiled around her middle.

While her drive had given her a measure of peace, she hadn't made any decisions regarding

Seth. She loved him and wouldn't deny it. The question was could she conquer her self-esteem issues with Seth's help the way she'd conquered her fear of intimacy? Would Seth understand what it was like growing up never feeling good enough to warrant the "right" kind of love? Better yet, did her feelings for Seth revolve around the gratitude she accused him of feeling for her? Gratitude because he'd helped her through such a difficult time?

No. She loved him. That much she knew for sure. But the last thing she wanted was for her insecurities with herself, her self-image, to remain a barrier between them. Which meant she had to voice her fears about their relationship aloud to Seth, and also ask that he explain his feelings for Arie. Sharing, openness, honesty. All things her counselor said were a must when dealing with issues like hers.

The news reports put such a heroic slant on her helping Lexi out of the rafters and her battle with Roy that she had requests for interviews and several job offers sight unseen. She had one huge decision to make. Seth had regained sensation in one leg, and could sense tingles and pricks in his other foot. It wouldn't be long before he recovered completely. He wouldn't need her PT services anymore and that would free both of them to deal with their feelings…one way or the other.

A knock sounded at the door. Grace opened her

blurred eyes, hoping the person didn't expect her to get up, because after all the activity she'd had today it wasn't going to happen.

"You okay, Grace?" he asked through the door.

"Yeah, Brent, I'm fine. But I don't want to talk," she answered, knowing without a doubt her brother would understand. A scratch came from the floor a split second before Blackie jumped to her lap and made herself at home.

She rubbed the ears of the rapidly growing kitten, smiling when its purr resembled a motor. "What do you think I should do?"

"Talk to me," Seth murmured from behind her. He wheeled himself inside the door separating their bedrooms and shut it behind him. "I heard what you told Brent," he said, rolling closer until he sat beside her. Blackie blinked at Seth, then took off with a haughty sniff and twitch of her tail. "But I also remember telling you to go away and you came in, anyway." He snagged her hand and held it between both of his. "Shows you. I can be stubborn, too." His expression softened, his worry painfully evident. "You disappeared on me."

"I needed some time."

He raised her hand and kissed her knuckles. "I remember that, too. I tried to get everyone to leave me alone, even though I needed someone to talk to. Just like I think you need me now."

Her nose tingled with the threat of tears. "I...I went to Earl's grave." Seth looked surprised and she smiled, her head lolling on the recliner's back. "I had to vanquish his demon. And I think I may have managed it. To some extent, anyway."

"I'm glad."

She looked down at their clasped hands. "And I'm confused."

He leaned closer. "I love you. Whatever you're confused about, we'll work through it."

She inhaled as deeply as was possible, given her ribs, and moaned. *Just say it. See what he says. Don't be a coward.*

"Did you hear Phil Estes talking to me in the kitchen?"

What did Phil have to do with Seth loving her? "Something about a project."

Seth tilted his head to one side. "Brent's moving into the bunkhouse as soon as he finishes college."

"What? But—why would he stay here?"

Seth's frown indicated his disappointment in her words. "He's created a lot of his inventions to help people like me," he explained, "so why not let him showcase his work at a ranch dedicated to giving children, teens, adults—whoever—the chance to use them?"

"I don't understand." Oh, but even her medicated mind was beginning to make sense of his words. His *project.* That was how Seth was going to save his ranch. And Brent would help. Brent loved Montana and had always talked about moving back.

"I hate the name 'dude' ranch, but in this case it fits. Phil's helping me turn my ranch into a place for special-needs families. A place where wheelchair ramps are the norm, not the exception. Thanks to the ideas Brent's come up with, guests will be able to ride and fish, snowmobile, whatever—comfortable that every possible consideration has been given to their disability."

"Wow."

Seth grinned. "Yeah. I think it's pretty incredible myself. Phil said the grants are going smoothly. He's never seen anything like it. Government agencies want to give us money, private organizations want to send people here to help set it all up at no cost. There's nothing like it in this part of the country and everyone's wanting to get in on it. It's amazing."

"It sounds…wonderful." It was more than wonderful. It was fantastic. And she wasn't surprised at all Seth had come up with something so unique given the problems he'd had adjusting.

"Maura's agreed to be our chef. She's missed cooking all those fancy meals, so a few nights a week she's going to go all out. She and Jake are going to stay on in the house while they build a place of their own. Maura also has a cousin who's going to be the housekeeper and help out with the babies. She has a girl with some problems and wants to get out of the city where they live now, so she's going to use the studio. Everything's falling into place except for one thing—we need a full-time physical therapist to care for the guests."

A full-time therapist. *Here?* She shook her head dazedly, unable to take it all in. Her head ached, her ribs ached and she wanted to say yes more than anything. "Are you still in love with Arie?" There, it was out. And now that it was she couldn't look at him. She hadn't meant to blurt it out like that but—

Seth leaned over and turned her face to his with a hand under her chin. "No, I'm not," he denied firmly. "I thought you knew by now that you're the only woman I love. Have ever loved. Why would you think otherwise?"

"You won't talk to me about her and…"

"And what?"

She found it hard to swallow. "I worry that our feelings for each other aren't entirely…honest."

"Meaning yours?"

Somewhat defensive, she shrugged. "And yours. You won't talk about Arie. I've asked you, remember?"

Seth smoothed his free hand roughly over his

face and grimaced. "Ah, Grace, I don't know how to….you're wrong, honey. I didn't love Arie."

"But you married her."

"Yes, I did," he agreed with a nod. "And I cared for her in the beginning, but at the end when she died—" His expression darkened. "All I felt was relief."

Shock was the norm for the past few days and now was no exception. "But…you can't bear to have her paintings in the house. Won't speak of her. Because it's so painful."

"And you're comparing yourself to her," he murmured knowingly. "Sweetheart, don't. Please don't. There is no comparison—don't look at me like that either. Let me explain. I don't talk about Arie because her death was painful." Seth lifted her hand to his lips again, kissing it before mouthing the words against her fingers. "Maura had recently found out she was pregnant with Lex. I knew something was going on because Jake was acting weird and talking about dropping out of college. Anyway, I went up to see them, we worked out a plan, I met Arie and…two weeks after that, Arie announced she was pregnant as well.

"I never doubted her. Never thought it might be a lie. Arie was extremely…emotional. She seemed all right most of the time, but then something would trigger her and she'd go off. And I can't be entirely sure, but I think she made up the pregnancy, probably because she was jealous of all the attention Maura was getting from their family. Maura and Jake planned a small ceremony, bought the white dress and a cake. Arie had to have that, too, only bigger and better. Then, when she should've been showing and wasn't, I confronted her, tried to get her to go to the doctor. She put me off with excuses for a while, but then she finally said she'd lost the baby."

"Oh, Seth."

"At that point Maura only had a year or so left of schooling to become a chef, so Arie volunteered to watch Lexi and even claimed it helped her cope with losing our baby. I still didn't doubt her story, and with Jake and Maura both in school, I didn't argue, either. But sometimes I'd walk in and Lexi would be screaming and Arie—" he released a gruff curse "—Arie would have her headset on to block out the noise, painting away, not even bothering to try to soothe Lexi."

His gaze met hers briefly before sliding away, and in that moment Grace saw Seth's insecurities, raw emotions just below the surface. She connected with him in that instant, knew she wasn't alone. "I left one morning to go bring in some of the horses before a storm hit. With so many people in the house, I'd hired Hank's wife to come and give Arie a hand with the baby and cleaning, but that day she was late. In the rush I forgot something and had to turn around, but when I got back to the house…" He inhaled roughly. "Something was wrong. I *knew* it. I ran inside, expecting Lexi to be crying, but everything was quiet. So I went up to Lexi's room to check on her, and found Arie standing over her bed with a knife in her hands, ready to plunge it into Lex."

Grace gasped, her hand jerking up to cover her mouth.

"I lunged for her, we fought. She tried to stab me, but I got the knife away from her. She screamed obscenities, told me she hated me and the ranch and everyone on it. Then she took off. Her car slammed into a tree about a mile outside town." Seth raised his gaze to hers. "When I told Jake—"

"He was furious," she murmured. "That's why he won't move into the studio, isn't it? Because it was hers and she—"

Seth nodded.

"But Maura—after all this time how does she not know? She's never said a word about this."

His mouth firmed. "I left it up to Jake to tell her, but he hasn't. Maura blamed me for letting Arie drive when she was that angry and upset, but—I can't blame Jake. How do you tell someone the sister she'd finally grown to love had tried to kill her baby? Jake doesn't want Maura to know how much Arie hated her. How twisted she was. He says there's no need when it would only bring more hurt to her and her family. Especially since Jake and I think Arie slammed into the tree on purpose."

Grace moaned softly at the image his words evoked. "Oh, Seth. I'm so sorry. I had it wrong all this time."

Seth stroked her cheek, mindful of the bruise. "I *didn't* love her, Grace. To this day I can't get the picture of her out of my head. The knife, Lexi so close to death. Thank God Lex was asleep and never saw a thing."

"Unlike you. You lived the nightmare."

His eyes were bleak as he nodded. "As did you. Earl's abuse has made you question your feelings for everything and everyone, hasn't it?"

Seth leaned forward until his forehead rested against hers. "What I feel for you isn't gratitude. After all that happened with Arie, I know the difference between love and infatuation, and I love you, Grace. *You.*"

Tears slipped out before she could stop them. "I love you, too. I'm sorry."

"Then marry me."

"Seth, you have to understand—the nightmares, my past, all of this with Roy. It might not be over." She moaned softly. "It might never go away completely. The insecurity, the doubts. I'm determined to accept that it happened and move on, but it isn't going to happen overnight—it may take years and who knows if I'll ever let go completely.

"I don't care. Things like this aren't meant to be dealt with alone. You trusted me enough to tell me, now trust me enough to help you. With your determination and my stubbornness, we'll make it, Grace." His nose brushed hers in a near kiss. "We'll weather it together."

Hope soared through her, but so did fear. "Are you sure you're not simply trying to get a free therapist?"

He pressed a kiss to her mouth, sweet, lingering. "You'll get all the fringe benefits."

"And those are?"

"Depends. Is that a yes?"

She paused, drawing out the moment until Seth's gaze narrowed and he kissed her again as though *that* were punishment. She laughed softly, happier than she'd ever been in her life.

"Yes," she murmured, her lips firm against his. "I'll be your…therapist."

EPILOGUE

Six months later

GRACE HADN'T PLANNED on being a June bride, but when Seth set his mind to something, she'd learned he generally got his way. She took a deep breath, conscious of everyone's eyes on her as she exited the house with Brent at her side, her hand on his arm as they walked down the aisle toward the garden where the ceremony would take place.

She spotted Seth standing beneath the decorated arbor, handsome in his tux and western string tie. She'd never seen him in formal dress. Not even when the ranch officially opened its doors for business two months earlier after a whirlwind of activity and building to accommodate their physically limited guests.

Seth leaned heavily on the cane in his hand, but when their eyes met, he straightened, a smile curving his lips up.

He'd been impatient to get married immediately,

but as he wanted to stand during the ceremony, he'd agreed to her request to wait long enough to heal and cope with not only Roy's attack, but with all the changes taking place in her life.

Two weeks earlier Roy had been sentenced to prison for attempted rape, assault and every other charge that could be thrown his way. His prison term wasn't a long one, but at least he was gone and would now have a record following his release.

As she watched, Seth's expression filled with love, and he was uncaring that nearly all of North Star watched. He winked at her and nudged Jake, murmuring something that made both men grin and more than one woman in the crowd smile in response, including Maura, her matron of honor. Jake and Maura's baby boys were propped up by pillows as they were pulled up the aisle in front of her in a decorated wagon led by Lexi. Even Blackie was dressed for the occasion, the all-white cat sported a soft pink bow that matched Lexi's dress.

When Grace was at Seth's side, she accepted his extended hand, sighing at the love and support she found in his eyes.

Their gazes locked firmly on each other, she and Seth vowed before God and their family and friends to love each other for the rest of their lives, to battle through the hard times and relish the good. Side by side.

Grace didn't believe it was possible to feel so exposed, so vulnerable, and yet so happy while she bared her heart and soul to everyone present.

"You may kiss your bride."

With a wicked grin and promise in his eyes, Seth tossed his cane to Jake and cradled her face in his hands, raising her mouth to his. Their lips met, held in a sweet, soft caress that deepened to the delight and cheers of the crowd.

"Ladies and gentlemen, may I present for the very first time, Mr. and Mrs. Seth Rowland of the Second Chance Ranch!"

HARLEQUIN *Super*ROMANCE®

**A powerful new story from a
RITA® Award-nominated author!**

A Year and a Day
by **Inglath Cooper**

**Harlequin Superromance #1310
On sale November 2005**

Audrey Colby's life is the envy of most. She's
married to a handsome, successful man, she
has a sweet little boy and they live in a lovely
home in an affluent neighborhood. But
everything is not always as it seems. Only
Nicholas Wakefiled has seen the danger
Audrey's in. Instead of helping, though,
he complicates things even more....

Available wherever Harlequin books are sold.

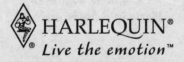

HARLEQUIN®
Live the emotion™

www.eHarlequin.com   HSRAYAD1105

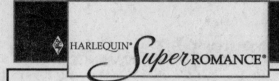

HARLEQUIN *Super*ROMANCE®

HOMETOWN
+U.S.A.+

An Unlikely Match
by **Cynthia Thomason**

Harlequin Superromance #1312
On sale November 2005

She's the mayor of Heron Point. He's an
uptight security expert. When Jack Hogan
tells Claire Betancourt that her little town
of artisans and free spirits has a security
problem, sparks fly! Then her daughter goes
missing, and Claire knows that Jack is the
man to bring her safely home.

Available wherever
Harlequin books are sold.

HARLEQUIN®

AMERICAN *Romance*®

Presenting…

CHRISTMAS, TEXAS STYLE

A holiday gift for readers of
Harlequin American Romance

Novellas from three of
your favorite authors

Four Texas Babies
TINA LEONARD

A Texan Under the Mistletoe
LEAH VALE

Merry Texmas
LINDA WARREN

*Available November 2005 wherever
Harlequin books are sold.*

The long walk home to what matters most is worth every step.

Three very different women learn to bridge the generation gap that separates them and end up becoming closer than ever.

A LONG WALK HOME

DIANE AMOS

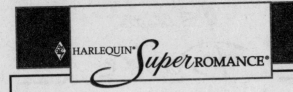

HARLEQUIN *Super* **ROMANCE**

Critically acclaimed author

Tara Taylor Quinn

brings you

The Promise of Christmas

Harlequin Superromance #1309
On sale November 2005

In this deeply emotional story, a woman
unexpectedly becomes the guardian of her
brother's child. Shortly before Christmas,
Leslie Sanderson finds herself coping with
grief, with lingering and fearful memories and
with unforseen motherhood. She also
rediscovers a man from her past who could
help her move toward the promise
of a new future....

Available wherever Harlequin books are sold.

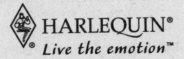

HARLEQUIN®
Live the emotion™